Earning Innocence

Earning Innocence

A NOVEL

Andrew Taylor-Troutman

RESOURCE *Publications* · Eugene, Oregon

EARNING INNOCENCE
A Novel

Resource Publications
An Imprint of Wipf and Stock Publishers
199 W. 8th Ave., Suite 3
Eugene, OR 97401

www.wipfandstock.com

ISBN 13: 978-1-4982-3153-4

Manufactured in the U.S.A.   10/13/2015

For my mom, Anna Troutman
"A book about relationships & redemption for those who seek
to build relationships & who have been redeemed."

There is an earned innocence, I believe, which is as much to be honored as the innocence of children.

—Reverend John Ames from Marilynne Robinson's *Gilead*.

Contents

An Author's Note

All of the characters, scenes, vignettes, and experiences of *Earning Innocence* are products of the play of my imagination. And I have had a lot of fun!

Sometimes these fictional people flirt, sing, laugh, and pray in "real" places, i.e., somewhere a reader might have the opportunity to go and do likewise. In the novel, however, those experiences are not meant to be representational of actual locations or institutions—except in the way, of course, that fiction mirrors life. Specifically, there is a town of Talmage outside Philadelphia—no part of this manuscript was meant to depict this fine locale or its magnanimous people, either in August of the year of Our Lord 2000 or at any other time in history. One final caveat: the opinions expressed here are not intended to represent those of any baseball player, funeral home director, retired military officer, folk singer, Floridian, librarian, Border collie, or pastor of any denomination—except in the way, of course, that fiction speaks our truth for us.

The novel, however, does intentionally and unabashedly echo my deep, *deep* abiding and loving appreciation for Marilynne Robinson's *Gilead*. In addition, certain characters occasionally make remarks quite similar to something I have heard or read elsewhere. So I wish to acknowledge my debt to Nadia Bolz-Weber for the idea of scars and wounds and to Ann Lamott's mother's big black pocketbook. The late David Foster Wallace once uttered a memorable riff on Jesus and the truth setting you free. Richard Lischer played Burnout with his son, Adam. The image of a husband and wife racing from bed to the kitchen each morning is from Elizabeth Dark Wiley's award-winning essay, "If You Want It To Last" (*Ruminate*, Issue 35: summer, 2015). I acknowledge and thank Brian Doyle for the hint of a hint of a smile and many other melodious phrases I unconsciously borrowed from drinking great gulps of his writing—see what I did there? And there are images in *Earning Innocence* that are borrowed from enlightened sources. The story of Jacob and the blessing limping forward is found in the Book of Genesis. The ancient rabbis, who knew the power of this and other stories, compared a parable to a candlewick. The image of a teenage son giving his father a halfway hug is from Brock Clarke's "Good Night" (*The Sun*: May, 2015). His short story, not more than a single paragraph, has haunted me in the very best of ways.

Like Bonnie Wheeler, I am indebted to a group of intelligent truth-telling women who gave of their talent and time in support of my goal: Marjorie Stelmach was my first reader, a mentor who coached, challenged, and cheered; Heather Vacek offered a historian's perspective as well as deft plot analysis; Claire Asbury Lennox thoroughly and astutely marked up a first draft—I owe you some more red pens; Katherine Bowers, Angela Alaimo O'Donnell, and Mary Howard Shaw each gave sharp insights and welcomed affirmations; Jane Willan breathtakingly cut the entire original opening and helped me to breathe deeply while making down-to-the-wire tweaks, which may well make all the difference. Rocky Supinger is a dude, of course, but was helpful in his delightful Yo-Rocko way. And my beloved, Ginny, is steadfast loving kindness—*chesed* in the original biblical language. I give thanks for this communion of the mind. My gratitude to each one of you is indescribable.

This book is dedicated to my mom, Anna Troutman, who once wrote on the inside cover of Paul Harding's *Tinkers*: "A book about relationships & redemption for those who seek to build relationships & who have been redeemed."

Mom gave me that book with inscription as a birthday present in January, 2011. I have wanted to write a story worthy of that blessing ever since.

And Sam, Daddy is finished working now. Yes, Daddy is all done. Do you want to read a book?

August 12th, 2000

"Jaime, there will be time for that later."

Bonnie's voice is my clarion call. She knows better than anyone why I need to sit here and write. But right now she is pouring bubbly in the other room. Do not over think this one, Wheeler!

Time to go.

August 13th, 2000

Bonnie has gone to bed, but I must record the events of today.

Today was our twenty-eighth wedding anniversary.

A remarkable sentence. Married at the age of nineteen, my head full of hair, empty of knowledge. Married with Bonnie's pregnancy clearly showing, full of promise.

We toasted each other last night from that bottle of relatively expensive champagne. On this bright morning, I paused to kiss my beloved at the front door before heading to church like I always do. As I turned to walk away, she gave me a playful squeeze through the seat of my dress pants. I had a spring in my step as I traveled the short distance down the gravel road to the sanctuary.

During August here in eastern Pennsylvania, even the songbirds are drained from the heat, their morning hymns weary and listless. Yet I knew Bonnie would skip into our kitchen, her smile still radiant. Leaving the dirty dishes from last night in the sink, she would sashay toward the pantry, fetching the organic flour, and then open the fridge, collecting farm fresh milk, eggs, butter. While wives of preachers across the country would adorn choir robes or chase kids around the nursery or fix yet another pot of decaf coffee, Bonnie Wheeler would cook for herself and for herself alone. Of course, she has done all of those duties and many more over the years. But today, on our twenty-eighth wedding anniversary, she would whip up *crepes Suzette*. Not only would she add Grand Marnier liqueur to the batter, she would take extra sips from the bottle. Whisk flour, eggs, and extra sugar together. Stir in milk and vanilla with fresh orange zest. Miles Davis on the stereo, her absolute favorite sacred artist. Pausing in the middle of the quiet tree-lined road on my way to work, I could hear the music in my head. I could envision her pajama-bottomed behind swaying in time with the down beat.

I have always resisted the metaphor of ordination as marriage to the church. Perhaps the Bard was correct: *he doth protest too much.* I had no intentions of any ministry when I met Bonnie. I had no idea of much of anything—except that she fascinated me. That much has not changed over the years. As my waistline has expanded and my hairline receded, I have felt a tug toward writing an account of my life here at this desk before this open window. Tonight, the fireflies flicker their love songs above the stalks of corn. What light might I share?

The good people of Talmage Moravian Church were aware of the significance of this day in my life. Many smiled and offered congratulations as we mingled in the sanctuary before the start of the service. There have been receptions after worship, which I always found a bit embarrassing. I suppose I am an unusual pulpiteer in this regard, but I have never cared for the spotlight. Now that Bonnie takes this Sunday off from church and our sons have left home, I am grateful for the lack of personal attention in more ways than one. It affords the opportunity to remind these Moravians of a much older anniversary.

The thirteenth of August marks one of the two chief festival days unique to our denomination. We share high holy days, like Easter and Pentecost, with the rest of the Christian world. But we also recall the story of refugees, fleeing religious persecution, who were invited to settle on the estate of Count Nikolaus Ludwig von Zinzendorf. My boys have referred to him as the Z-man since they were in middle school. A sign of disrespect? I confess I rather like that nickname, perhaps because I started attending church when I was a teenager.

Born into a wealthy noble family, the Z-man was by all accounts a precocious child and the legends surrounding his youth are numerous and dramatic, if not apocryphal. My favorite is that he allegedly wrote detailed love letters to Christ at the age of six, for my sons used to scribble letters to Jesus on the back of their Sunday morning bulletins when they were about that age. I have kept a few. Philip once scrawled his self-portrait alongside a tall, bearded man whom he labeled as *My Bestest Pal*. In slightly smaller font underneath, he included the subscript *Not my brother*. Let the record show.

As for that older brother, Nathaniel had a habit of writing to Jesus with his Christmas wish list—an understandable mistake in this consumer crazy culture. But he pledged in ink that, if Jesus would give him a hundred dollars, he would then tithe to the poor. The boy drew up a rudimentary contract and left the signed document in the offering plate.

In the early decades of the eighteenth century, Moravian refugees were granted land on the Zinzendorf Estate in which to establish a town they christened Herrnhut, which means The Lord's Watch. This name asserts unity and common purpose. Only five years later, the community threatened to divide. A carpenter by the name Christian David turned fiery preacher and built unrest with his end-of-times predictions. I am reminded of the so-called prophets predicting doom over something known as Y2K. If the sad history of religious power struggles within the church and surrounding culture teaches us anything, it is to be wary of those calling themselves "Christian" and acting completely otherwise.

By contrast, we would do well to learn from the Z-man's example. He had already retired from civic duties in order to immerse himself in Bible study and theology. He then devoted his time toward healing the fractured community, traveling to each family's home to pray together and stress the love of Christ for all. As the fruit of such tireless efforts, the whole community gathered on the thirteenth of August in the year of Our Lord 1727 for a special Wednesday service of Holy Communion. According to several eye witness accounts, the Holy Spirit fell upon all those in attendance.

Known by historians as the Moravian Pentecost, the title sounds a little pompous to me. I think of Mother Mary and how she was "overshadowed" by the Spirit like a cloud passing over the land. The most mystical revelations are described by quite ordinary words. Grand titles are bestowed only later. The Z-man wrote of the experience as *a sense of the nearness of Christ* and added: *We had hardly known whether we'd been on earth or in heaven.*

Bonnie thinks that last statement is rather erotic. I failed to mention this from the pulpit this morning.

Every congregation in our denomination tells the story of the thirteenth of August and celebrates Communion on the Sunday closest to the date. As part of this remembrance, we hear the Scripture about the bread that was broken and the cup that was poured. Grafted onto the vine of Israel and the Church Universal, we proclaim God's gracious redemption with thanksgiving, recalling love meals where no one should ever be forgotten. More Christians should believe that we are what we eat. Body and spirit are as inseparable in a breathing soul as the ingredients in a loaf of baked bread or *crepes Suzette*. This is white magic, as Bonnie used to say to our boys.

I have stood at the Lord's Table here at Talmage Moravian Church for nineteen years now. Though I am a short man whose glasses only adequately compensate for severe near-sightedness, I still have the best views.

Earlier today, in the year of Our Lord 2000, I invited all baptized adults and confirmed members to partake together. Like most congregations, we ask seekers to participate in a period of religious education before receiving the sacrament so that the meaning of the ritual is deepened. Typically, youth begin confirmation class at twelve years, going on thirteen. But who are we to prevent someone from receiving the gifts of God? I happened to see a toddler named Jacob remove the lollipop from his mouth with one hand and nibble an unleavened wafer in the other, before returning the rest to his grandmother with sticky fingers and bright eyes. Behind them, an elderly couple chewed together. I knew that even Ralph Jibsen's jaws had been weakened from the cancer treatments. Sharing bread of the same body, I prayed silently for them as Ralph eased an emaciated arm across the healthy shoulders of his beloved of forty years.

My gaze wandered to a youth sitting directly above their heads in the balcony, a twelve-year-old boy who is the only student in this year's confirmation class. Charlie was holding the hand of a girl about his age. Even as I write this memory, I am smiling at their innocence. I have never seen her before, but have known Charlie since the day he was born two months premature and resembled a tiny spider monkey.

After we had eaten as one, the trays bearing cups of salvation were likewise distributed to the people in the pews. Everyone sang hymns of praise and petition. Marjorie Stemlich skillfully played the treble line with one hand, accepted the juice with the other, and rested the tiny cup on top of the piano, never missing a note. Frank Powers sat in the pew closest to her. He shakily removed his little plastic cup from the silver serving tray and gripped this small vessel of grace with both trembling hands—determined to hold on to his dignity, even as Parkinson's grabs more of him.

Patsy Miller worshipped in the first pew, exact center of the sanctuary. She is stone-faced throughout every Sunday service. She recently confided that she still senses her husband's presence next to her in the pew. It has been five years. In moments of painful absence, she thinks of the readings at Brother Stanley's funeral, which promised a day when there will be no more hunger or thirst or pain or suffering or grief or death ever again. *No, not ever again,* I thought, and lifted my cup to my lips in unison with Sister Patsy and the rest of the believers both seen and unseen.

Glancing along the back wall, I was just in time to spot a mischievous nine-year-old point his bony elbow at his seven-year-old brother's ribs and launch a surprise attack, swiftly jabbing at the exact moment his victim had intended to swallow. Poor brother spat the blood of forgiveness across his lap. Ben and Michael are good boys, joyfully wild in that not-entirely-restrained way afforded by trusting parents. Steve and Betsy had waited a long, long time for those boys, enduring several miscarriages.

Miscarriages. Lord have mercy.

I made sure to tell Bonnie that Betsy had been in worship. The Lewis family attends sporadically, which has put more distance between Steve and me. But our wives have remained close. They have shared tea together every month since Bonnie discerned

Betsy's infertility troubles from a friend of a friend's insensitive comment in the church parking lot. Often the cup we share is one of sorrow. But there is a red hymnal in their pew marked with an even redder streak across a portion of the Communion liturgy, the telltale stain of horseplay when my boys were about that age, fidgety and mischievous in the exact same pew. Indeed, there is mercy.

Both of my sons are hanging out between semesters, working a little, and mostly doing God-only-knows-what since they do not tell their father. Though away for the summer, they are remembered by many of the faithful sprinkled throughout the sanctuary on Sunday mornings. These witnesses likewise recall that Communion service long ago when a homeless man received the elements with the rest of us and then shuffled slowly down the aisle, departing without a word. He was never seen again, though I think of him often. That was the first time I ever presided alone at the Lord's Table. And the keepers of this church's memory preserve the saga of the gold-plated cross gracing the Lord's Table, which once went missing for months on end and was presumed lost forever until finally discovered in a small cave less than a mile away by a group of children playing Peter Pan and the Lost Boys. No questions were asked, which might represent the difference between mercy and grace.

I happened to notice Jacob's grandmother offer the remains of her cup to the same sticky fingers. About a year ago, I baptized this little boy in this very sanctuary. How he had cried! More than a few people have reminded me of this fact with a quiet hand on my shoulder and the hint of a hint of a smile. Jacob accepted the drink with quiet reverence during today's sacrament. But then he declared in his high-pitched voice, "Yes, yes, yes, yes!"

Yes, indeed. I felt a sense of the nearness of Christ.

When I returned home, I found Bonnie wrapped up in her favorite blanket on the living room couch with about a third of the bottle of liqueur. She was poring through one of our oldest family photo albums. I made a pot of tea and joined her, my entrance perfectly timed to appreciate her soft sigh of wonder at one of our favorite images of all time. It is of Nathaniel, our first baby boy, asleep on my chest on another Sunday afternoon. His scrunched up newborn face is slack with utter contentment, his drool pools on my freshly starched shirt. In unison, we quote the doctor's first words when Nathaniel James Wheeler came into this world.

"What a handsome boy!"

We flipped the page and there he is again, sitting on top of his first bicycle, the one with a yellow seat shaped like a banana. And there he is at his high school graduation, wearing that funny-looking square hat, a noticeable redness on his neck from that morning's razor burn. Nathaniel paused on stage after receiving his diploma and turned to face the audience. He refrained from show-boating unlike some of the other graduates who made outlandish gestures for shock effect or applause. I admire the way my son savored the moment.

Having zoomed through his life, I fetched the twin album that bore the images of our second child. Bonnie in the hospital bed, smiling wearily. We heard that the second one was easier, but she labored twice as long. From the day he was born, Philip has had a full head of dark hair like his mother. Her green eyes, too. In the next picture, our new baby lies on the couch beside his brother and Nathaniel's mouth hangs open wide as if in amazement. Yet another of both boys, each wearing a Pirates baseball cap. Pittsburgh has always been our team. Squinting at this fading photo, I can barely distinguish a white blur suspended between Nathaniel's empty hand and Philip's outstretched glove. They were five and three because that was our first spring at Talmage Moravian. The sanctuary is visible behind them, which was true for most of their lives.

Now that both are in college, Philip no longer attends church and Nathaniel volunteers with a ministry for high school students.

I believe my sons share many of the same ideological commitments; yet they have increasingly crossed swords, clashing during heated dinner conversations and angry phone calls. Sometimes I tell Bonnie this is just another phase, which they will grow out of soon enough like bed-wetting or smoking marijuana. Sometimes I even believe myself.

I do not believe I have been helpful in these matters of dispute. I am prone to defend Nathaniel's position, which is often in defense of the church, specifically, and the way they were raised, implicitly.

It helps to remember one late summer evening when the boys were in high school and the three of us were fishing in the little pond behind the church. There are no pictures, but I can clearly remember how the weather was unusually cool, not the least bit humid, and how the reds and oranges and pinks of the setting sun were like streaks of paint across the surface of the water's canvas. But the language of both boys was like ugly graffiti scrawled across a moral landscape. I forget what they were arguing about. I only know that my offspring ignored my plea for peace and quiet, completely impervious to my stated desire. This only made me madder, naturally. But Philip suddenly let out a whoop of excitement. His pole was being pulled out of his hands.

Part of me hoped the catch would turn out to be an old boot or something—a mirage instead of miracle. Despite myself, I shared their excitement as Philip reeled and pulled, fighting whatever it was for all it was worth. As much as we fished, we rarely caught anything. Both boys followed in their father's footsteps in this regard. Philip finally reeled the fish over to where we were standing on the bank. With a dramatic tug, he pulled it up and out of the water. I watched the squiggly silver projectile sail through the air and land with a *thump* on the bank, right in the middle of all three of us.

"Wow! Look at that! Amazing!"

They had forgotten their age and how nothing was supposed to impress them. And I had to admit this catch was worthy of exclamation. This is no fisherman's tale: it weighed at least eight, maybe ten pounds and upon closer inspection was covered in bright colors cascading down both its sides. As it flipped and flopped on the green grass, the fish blurred bright like a kaleidoscope. For a few moments, we all watched in silence.

"Let's throw it back," Nathaniel declared. For once, Philip nodded in agreement. Both of them bent down together, working in concert, as Philip held the fish still while Nathaniel eased the hook from its mouth, careful to minimize the damage. He nodded at his brother. Four hands lifted the catch and lowered it back into the pond.

Bonnie would have appreciated that memory. But slightly buzzed and full of her *crepes Suzette*, she had drifted off to sleep on the couch. After gently transferring her head from my shoulder to a pillow, I decided to drive to the Pleasant Shade Senior Living Community and offer Communion to those who could not attend this morning's service. Sunday is Sunday, anniversary or not.

Entering the lobby, I noticed an elderly resident slumped in a wingback chair. I assumed he was asleep, his eyes hidden underneath his American flag ball cap, until he jerked his cane toward my Communion set.

"Son, what the hell you got in there?"

I showed him, opening the dark red box emblazoned with a silver cross.

"You let me get some for myself!"

I smiled through gritted teeth. There are a number of Moravians living at Pleasant Shade, and I was in a hurry to serve all of them and return home. But who was I to refuse anyone Communion, even a rude old man? I pulled up a chair next to him. Handing him an unleavened wafer the size and shape of a coin, I had intoned the ancient words *do this in remembrance of me* when he interrupted.

"I was in the shit! The shit, I tell ya!"

I am accustomed to parishioners taking the offering and slipping it wordlessly into their mouths, bowing their heads in solemn mastication. This strange old man kept cursing. He had another story to remember.

Before shipping off to war, his high school sweetheart had given him a Saint Christopher necklace. "They was having carnal

relations," as his mother of now blessed memory had once put it
to her nosy neighbor while her only son was still within earshot.
This sweetheart was, shall we say, superstitious. She knew all about
many different saints but, in particular, this Christopher—a broad-
shouldered, hulking bear of a man who had been poised to cross
a swiftly moving river, when a small child begged pitifully to be
carried to the other side. Obligingly, Christopher put the child on
his shoulders and discovered, much to his surprise, that this little
boy was incredibly heavy, so unbelievably burdensome because he
bore the sins of the whole world. Christopher became a saint by
carrying the Christ.

The old man told me how he had teased his girlfriend.

"You sure that's not just some of the Pope's mumbo-jumbo?"

Undaunted and undeterred, she had insisted upon placing the
necklace with its medal into his palm, closing his other hand over
top, pressing the cold metal to his flesh with whispered conviction.

"He's the saint of all travelers."

In the lobby of Pleasant Shade, he yanked off his hat and insisted he had not been religious at all—the Lord as his witness! By
God, he wanted me to understand that! He was young and strong.
He was brave and brash. He showed no damn weakness. He sure
as hell didn't need a savior, much less anyone's mumbo-jumbo. But
what did he have to lose?

He wore the metal around his neck every goddamn day of
his time in the shit, including the day when a bomb burst out of
nowhere, instantly killing his two best friends and knocking him
to the hard ground. Even before opening his eyes, his trembling
hands felt all over his body for wounds. Fearing the worst, he dared
to look.

"And there it was. The blessed thing was lying in the mud
right in front of me. I scooped it up and ran."

He then reached under his shirt and pulled out an old piece of
metal attached to a tarnished silver chain.

"Alright, Father, don't just sit there with your mouth agape
like a damn fish. Go ahead and serve the blessed wine."

I managed to stammer something about being addressed as "Pastor" because I was not Catholic, but Moravian.

"Mormon? What the hell?"

I assured him that Moravians were, in fact, Protestants and added that, actually, I had grape juice. I gave the plastic bottle a little shake to swirl the good old Welch's around.

"Ya damn Protestants," he sighed. "No wine and no saints."

When I came home for the second time on this my twenty-eighth anniversary, I found Bonnie talking to Philip on the phone. With a stern look, she handed me the receiver and mouthed *be nice*. She meant that she most certainly did not want me to pester him with a barrage of anxious questions concerning his specific behaviors over the past weekend. His twenty-first birthday is this Friday and Philip is coming home—provided that I do not jeopardize this precious opportunity ahead of time.

So I was very nice. In fact, I eagerly told Philip about the raw litany of the shit and Saint Christopher and so-called Mormons. The story prompted my youngest son's trademark laugh, a small chuckle so quiet it was barely audible over the phone. I knew, however, that his shoulders would have been shaking with mirth. There is a secret to quiet laughter, Abraham Lincoln once wrote. Picturing Philip, I reflected upon my son's life and what I know of his carnal relations and what I would give to protect him throughout his journey far from home. But I kept such thoughts to myself.

Philip wanted to know about Frank Powers, our old family friend who had recently moved to Pleasant Shade.

"Dad, you tell Mister Powers that I said I'm rooting for him, okay?"

I must try to remember, not only his words, but the sweetness of my son's voice as spoke.

If they know Moravians are not Mormons, most outsiders will think of us for our Lovefeasts at Christmas. Perhaps they are familiar with our sugar cakes and thin ginger cookies. We are most known for our baking, which I suppose is better than half-baked theology. But to be Moravian is to value a story. The story is the candlewick—common, ordinary, and hardly worth anything at all; yet the candlewick carries the light. This is cause for gratitude before bed. I will also offer prayers for traveling mercies.

August 14ᵗʰ, 2000

I have learned how to be an early riser. This is one of the lessons of parenthood. When we were first married, I would take afternoon classes in order to lounge in bed as long as possible. Children require a different schedule. I would be up with the boys, which meant changing diapers and pouring cereal, hunting socks from behind dressers and playing Hide-and-Seek, talking and tickling, laughing and listening. I am not complaining. These everyday tasks were sacraments, connecting us even in ways beyond our awareness. The ties that bind are mysterious. Grace is found in the ordinary ... if you are awake and paying attention.

Now my sons have outgrown our house, leaving me to take care of our dog.

Our Dylan is part Border collie, but has no interest in herding the likes of me, preferring to zigzag through the church's cemetery on our morning walk, apparently lured by all manner of smells, each one beyond my limited olfactory capabilities. Perhaps we are both searching. It is my mind that wanders through time and space as we meander through God's Acre. This is the traditional name given to each Moravian cemetery. Here at Talmage the grounds are actually more than an acre, but I absolutely believe these brothers and sisters belong to God.

According to our Moravian tradition, the gravestones are the exact same size, shape, and color, each an identical slab of white marble laid flat on the ground, inscribed with the person's name, dates of birth and death, and a single verse of scripture. Even a much smaller dog could clear one of our markers with an easy leap. There are financial reasons underpinning this arrangement, which belie the economic constraints of the early communities. More poignantly, tall and fancy tombstones were not only regarded as ostentatious, but as examples of worldly indulgence offensive to the Lord. Looking out on the rows of identical rectangles, one cannot help but feel a sense of the fundamental equality of all humankind—a belief I hold to be close to the heart of God. We are all brothers and sisters.

Walking Dylan can be a chore, yet I choose to spend precious free time among the markers of the dead. Standing before a loved one's tombstone, scraps of our conversations float to mind, bits and pieces of anecdotes, musings, questions. Faith. I have come to think of such fragmented recollections as prayer flags, colorful reminders of the unseen holy that passes through this world.

This very morning I noticed the grave of Paul Huxley, a friend who has been dead ten years. He came of age during the Great Depression, which indelibly marked many men and women of that generation. Along with other neighborhood children, Brother Paul used to chuck rocks at passing trains. "I had a good aim," he once told me with a shy smile. This often provoked engineers to hurl coal in apparent retaliation. But these conductors, whizzing past children on the wrong side of the tracks, offered lasting kindness in those fleeting moments. The kids would collect the bits of fuel in order to bring them back to their families and heat their homes. Unspoken covenants are sealed in the fires of need. I have preached on that story before, though I forget what I took as my text. Sometimes I just want to keep a legacy aflame.

A little on ahead, there lies Jerry Bentley, the man who every year happily completed our taxes, free of charge. God rest his soul. Brother Jerry added and subtracted, multiplied and divided without the use of a calculator. "I have more faith up here in my round noggin' than in any machine," he had a habit of saying while tapping the side of his head. Admittedly, that made me a little nervous. But the IRS never knocked on my door. And I can now recognize a kind of freedom that is becoming rare in our technological era.

Dylan and I stumble across a tombstone with the name Peter Davidson, though everyone knew our brother as Buster. He once described a dream about a swarm of bees chasing him, getting closer and closer. Unable to outrun them, he turned and pelted rocks in their direction, killing some, driving the rest away. This aggressive self-defense angered a massive bear who charged, snarling in rage. Buster threw and threw, but nothing slowed the revenge-seeking beast. "There could be no escape," he had whispered to me one quiet morning in my study at the church. Only a few weeks later, he was diagnosed with the inoperable, unstoppable brain tumor that snuffed his life much too soon.

I know without looking that Elmer Stetson is next to Buster. Though baptized Catholic, I never knew him to attend church regularly. I preached his service almost by default, as the man had no other pastor in his life. I became friendly with Brother Elmer because he would walk this very property and lob sticks into the adjoining woods, always with a sidearm throwing motion. I asked him about that once, and he explained he had shoulder problems. I got to know him a little better and he finally admitted, "I once pitched a little." Ever modest, he shrugged off my excitement. But I practically sprinted home to consult my copy of *The Baseball Encyclopedia*, a colossal tome that advertises itself as all-seeing as Homer and Milton and as all-knowing as Shakespeare and Yeats. I discovered Mr. Elmer Stetson had won thirty-five games and lost only seven for our Pittsburgh Pirates from 1926 to 1928. When Nathaniel and Philip discovered his true identity, they followed the old man around like he was the Pirates mascot, Captain Jolly Roger.

I ambled behind Dylan as she dashed past these graves and many more. Seems like every year I move a little slower, not due to aging, but rather on account of my habit of pausing before the tombstones that mark people I have loved. The number goes up all the time. I add the years written in stone between birth and death. Sometimes I scratch out the math in the freshly dug dirt with a stick. Then I launch my tool into the woods using a sidearm delivery. The dead fragments of the great living trees spin counter-clockwise through the air and settle to the ground once again. The past provides the material for the future.

Maybe I should preach about that.

I lingered for so long out there that Bonnie had already left for school by the time I returned home. She is the head librarian at the middle school because she is the only librarian at the middle school. Still, I am proud of her career. In addition to offering extra assistance to the students required to enroll for the summer, Bonnie spends the "off season" ordering a few new books and repairing many damaged old ones. She is well-versed in the art of book binding. Budget cuts to the public system wear on her, but Bonnie remains faithful. She, too, tends the stories, trimming the wicks that future generations might see by their light.

Without my beloved to share a morning cup of coffee, I called my best friend. McPherson answered on the second ring. He has been divorced for so long now that he says he might as well have been a lifelong bachelor. And he is always glad to meet me at Evy's Diner.

The Reverend Doctor Brian S. McPherson is a Presbyterian pastor and so very Presbyterian in his devotion to the original languages of the Bible. Like most of his denominational ilk, he is eager to drop this knowledge of Hebrew and Greek into every theological conversation.

"Wheeler, my good friend," he typically begins, pausing to rub his beard. "Wonder how that verse reads in the original?"

I took the same languages while at Moravian Seminary, but have not kept them up nearly as well. I have not kept them up at all. This is one of the many reasons to be grateful that I am not Presbyterian. Another would be John Calvin.

McPherson quotes John Calvin nearly as often as that other JC, the one known as *Yeshua* in one of the ancient languages. I have to admit that the theological forefather of the Presbyterians offers an occasional gem. He once said that every color in the world was given to proclaim God's glory. That is truly lovely, I readily concede. But as far as I can tell, the man spent far more time brooding and sulking.

McPherson jumps immediately to his hero's defense. Calvin's most infamous theory of total depravity is totally misunderstood, my friend argues nearly *ad nauseam*—this is especially true if you have just eaten his cooking. McPherson explains that it is not as though everything is depraved per se, but that sin touches every aspect of our lives, even our virtues. For example, Calvin insisted that total altruism is utterly impossible. Even when we try to be generous, our actions are tainted by self-centeredness and pride.

It is a wonder, then, that I offered to pick up the check for our coffees this morning.

The painter actually beat me to the church.

Due to my audience with McPherson, I arrived a little past nine and found a young man in his van, biding his time with the help of a cigarette. I led him inside and down the stairs into the fellowship hall. There, I was obliged to remain far longer than I had anticipated, as he kept picking up what might have been the tail end of our exchange of pleasantries, stringing along another question or comment to further the length of our conversation.

"So, what do you 'Mormons' believe, anyhow?"

I explained a little about Moravians, including our Z-man and the importance of the thirteenth of August. Perhaps we were both loitering. My schedule was clear. I thought I was going to have an easy day.

He painted as we chatted, returning his brush to the open bucket held in his other hand and then back to the wall, steadily layering fresh paint one smooth stroke at a time. Brush to bucket and back to wall, over and over again, as words passed between us. He eventually worked his way to confiding in me about his brother-in-law, a young man who died last Saturday while returning home from the second shift at the arsenal. Another driver under the influence had crossed the yellow line painted down the center of the road. Brush to bucket and back to wall—the painter told me about his sister, now a widow with a daughter set to enter kindergarten. What should he say? Did I have any advice? I watched him paint, striving to think of a sensitive response that would acknowledge his pain and perhaps point beyond it.

When Nathaniel was only two years old, he had drawn himself up to his full height and declared with righteous indignation, "I do not like words. Do not!" His mother and I were in the habit of spelling out certain terms to avoid confrontation like c-double-o-k-i-e. My son's comment was memorable because of the nature of my vocation. Whether spelled or spoken, sung or prayed, words are my medium. People look to me to paint, however imperfectly, some vision of the mysteries of life.

I shared with this painter that my mother had died in a car accident when I was twelve years old. There was nothing said for a long while after that.

Brush to bucket and back to wall.

He filled the silence, slapping some worn clichés in the space between us. Only the good die young; our loved ones are now in a better place; the sun dawns just before the darkest hour; God never gives us more than we can handle. He heard those words at the funeral, as part of the sermon. And he wanted to know what I preached about yesterday.

I told him a story of McPherson's about a particular children's sermon in which the pastor asked a half-circle of kids gathered in the front of the church, wiggling and squiggling before him in their Sunday best, what was grey and had a long tail and ate nuts and climbed trees. One little boy, suddenly stilled, his brow furrowed with concentration, raised his hand.

"Preacher, I know the answer supposed to be 'Jesus' but he sure sounds like a squirrel to me!"

After we had both laughed a little, I told him I was sorry for his loss, sorry for his sister and his niece. He nodded and resumed working. Brush to bucket and back to wall. I'll be praying for y'all, I added, judging by his accent that he was from the South. He smiled.

As I remember this exchange, I am thinking of all those prayers I have offered to God, Sunday after Sunday, every day of the week; all those words lifted up one at a time, over and over again. There are despairing moments in which they seem to cover nothing at all, much less someone's pain.

Yet when the painter stepped back to appraise his work, I sensed a sacred space had opened between us. That had sure felt like prayer to me.

The light plastic of the church's phone felt strangely heavy, as the news of Bud Thompson fell upon my ear. Dorothy had just learned of an explosion at Pleasant Shade involving her husband. She was desperately trying to find a babysitter. Could I go and be with Bud? Of course, I assured her, and promised to pray. As often happens, my petitions were interspersed with my memories. So much of prayer is a calling to mind.

On his feet all afternoon at his register, his bright smile ground into a tight-lipped grimace by the flood of inconsiderate shoppers, Bud crosses town in his equally exhausted old Honda in order to stand vigil at the night desk of the Pleasant Shade Senior Living Community. Everyone calls the place a "nursing" home, including the residents, which constantly serves to remind Bud of how his wife had left her job as an RN when their only child was born. Whenever I offer my sympathy regarding his grueling schedule, Bud holds up his hand, as if deflecting such sentiment.

"Pastor, it's all worth it. Every single minute of it."

The look on his face makes it clear. He means what he says. I admire this about Bud and have often made it a point to tell him while passing through his checkout line on my way home—a reality that has just as often tweaked my conscience.

Since he has to sleep at some point, Bud missed his two-year-old, haloed in soft morning light, lift his glass of milk and quite carefully pronounce, "I am a drinkin' sunshine." Dorothy tried to coax little Timothy into a second performance after his daddy had emerged from the dark lair of the bedroom. But some moments are tragically fleeting like the early rays themselves. And someone has to cover the rising cost of milk—even if the sunshine is free.

On this particular Monday morning, the day had announced its arrival with majestic red fanfare, which I had appreciated on my morning walk, having benefitted from a good night's sleep. But Bud had stared glassy-eyed at the same sunrise. At the end of an all-night shift on duty, on top of the previous day's work at the store, he had been so utterly consumed by his weariness that it took more than a few moments to register the flashing red button on the control panel beneath the window. When awareness finally dawned,

Bud had not been overly concerned as he was most often paged for quite pedestrian reasons, such as walking to a resident's room to fetch a glass of water.

But slogging through his fatigue, his senses were revived by the smell of smoke. The fire in the kitchen was rising from the stove, licking the ceiling with its tongues and snaking sideways across the countertop. An ancient and fragile woman crouched alone in the far corner, cowering with her knees pulled to her chest. Stooping to cradle her, Bud carried her to the safety of the hallway. As if transporting an infant to her crib, he gently set her down, whispering that everything would be all right. He had reentered the apartment to address the fire when the explosion hit.

After I found him in the burn unit, Bud told me the last thing he remembered was the heat like a punch in the face. At least that is what I thought he said. I was perched on the edge of his hospital bed, leaning forward and straining to hear. His shaky voice was muffled by the bandages covering the entire left side of his head.

We both sensed movement and simultaneously turned toward the door. Dorothy entered with Timothy in her arms. No luck finding a babysitter. I have always thought the child looked like a cherub—one of the chubby, ruddy-cheeked angels so popular on greeting cards. But his cheery face crumpled at the sight of his daddy. As Dorothy held Timothy's face tight to the V of her collarbone, she wordlessly sprinkled the crown of his head with tears. I felt like I should say something.

But Timothy suddenly jerked his head off his mother's chest and began to reach for Bud, wiggling so desperately that he threatened to spill right out of Dorothy's grasp like an armload of spaghetti. It was all she could do to set him down safely on the bed, as I stood and moved out of the way. Once there, Timothy's dark solemn eyes honed in upon what was wrapped around his daddy's head. Timothy punctured the silence.

"Daddy, you got toilet paper on your face!"

The visible portion of Bud's lips started to quiver. I could not tell if he was about to laugh or cry or some blessed combination thereof. The fingertips of his boy caressed those white wraps. Then that tiny hand found its way into his father's, and I watched half of Bud's face blossom into a goofy and joyous grin.

"Amen," exhaled Dorothy.

—•—

When I was in seminary, I occasionally asked my fellow students why they believed in God. Most of them stared at me blankly. How could they not believe in God? They were in seminary! They were baptized in the church and confirmed. They returned home from college for Christmas break and the Lovefeast buns never tasted so sweet. The church was what they knew. The church was all they knew.

I started going because I had nowhere else to go.

Late on the night my mom died, I waited until I was lying alone on my bed before sobbing, muffling the noise with a pillow over my face. I did not want Dad to hear; he was of no use to me. Finally, I seemed to have exhausted my supply of tears. I rolled off my bed and stretched across the floor, staring blankly at the ceiling.

And then, the light. A glowing from behind my eyes. But it was not blinding. Rather enveloping. And warm. So warm.

Then the words. Not audible, but in my mind.

Give it to me.

I bolted straight up like I had received an electric shock! And it happened once more.

Give it to me.

I crawled back in bed and immediately crashed into a deep, dreamless sleep.

I have since doubted this experience. Is "doubt" the right word? I have tried to rationalize that voice as my own projection, stemming from grief or loneliness or my father's lack of compassion or God knows what else. Anything else but God. I have tried to forget it ever happened or at least push the experience into the back of my mind. For periods of time, I have even convinced myself that it was all just a dream.

Give it to me.

I know that not everyone is blessed with such an experience. But I remembered those exact words again today as the hand of a tiny Christ reached into the beating heart of a hospital room. I can only add my Amen.

—•—

Lord, what a day. And it continued.

I had promised to accompany Bonnie on a visit to her dear friend's home that evening. Today was Wilma Sanderson's ninety-fourth birthday.

Over our nineteen years in this parish, Bonnie has befriended about a half dozen or so older women near the end of their lives. They had all been homemakers and mothers, every one of them conservative if not staunchly so. They were the kind of women who carried big black pocketbooks crammed full with Band-aids and snacks and lotions and sprays and Kleenex—everything one might need to take care of someone else. But what happens when even the grandchildren are grown and the only one left to take care of is you?

On one of our first visits with Sister Wilma, we lost track of the time. That evening was well over a decade ago because Bonnie had recently returned to graduate school. My wife said something to the effect that we hoped we had not kept our friend from other obligations. I have never forgotten the exact reply.

"Honey, I finished everything I *had* to do about twenty years ago."

Bonnie claims to be learning from such women how to become eccentric.

We arrived with the brownies and ice cream, fully intending a surprise. But the birthday girl flung open her apartment door while we were still making our way through the parking lot.

"Oh goody," she yelled down to us from the second floor. Just like her to use the word "goody" without sounding silly. She continued, "Guess what I did today?" Before giving us a chance to answer, she exclaimed, "I got my ears pierced!"

She rotated her head to the left and then the right and then back again. Even from a distance, the modest studs sparkled in the steamy fading light of summer.

At ninety four years, she still hustled us inside and launched into the play-by-play as we found seats in her cramped living room. The words tumbled out like a child rolling down a grassy hill. She had risen before sunrise, knowing what she wanted with crystal clarity, and had driven herself to the mall. Arriving before the stores

opened, there was nothing to do but wait, drumming her fingertips impatiently against the steering wheel until—oh goody—the
employees finally unlocked the doors. With the assistance of her
walker, she had propelled herself into the mall, thoroughly inspect-
ing not one but five kiosks, eventually returning to the first because
that particular employee had given her . . . good vibes.

I exchanged a look with Bonnie. Good vibes? Bonnie ignored
me. She had a more pressing question.

"Wilma, did it hurt?"

"Yes, honey, it sure did. But I was brave and now I'm beautiful!"

The story of her earring adventure completed, Sister Wilma
leaned back in her recliner, munching on one of her brownies, its
crumbs spilling down the front of her bathrobe. As an afterthought,
she casually mentioned that—oh-by-the-way—she had not taken
her medicine in over a week.

"Or, maybe it's ten days," she mused with a shrug. "I don't even
know!" She laughed boldly. "And you know what? I feel awesome!"

Wilma Sanderson wiggled her toes stretched out in front of
her and swallowed the remains of her birthday treat in one large
bite. She resumed playfully tugging at the studs in her ears—a
white-haired, wrinkly, wizened child of God.

On the drive home, I expressed my concerns to Bonnie. I knew
our friend had been forbidden by her doctor to drive, a prohibition
endorsed by her children. I maintained that no one should stop
their prescriptions without first receiving proper medical attention.

Bonnie shrugged.

"If you don't trust your good vibes, who will?"

A short while later, I had just finished telling my wife that she,
too, was brave and beautiful when we happened to pass the painter
on the gravel road from the church to our home. He flagged us
with a wave. I cranked the window down. The night air was finally
beginning to cool.

"All's finished," he said with a satisfied nod. He mentioned
that he had locked the church. I thanked him for his good work.
Our two vehicles idled in the road. He smashed his cigarette in the

ashtray. His tired work van coughed black smoke from the exhaust pipe.

"Pastor, you just don't stop praying, you hear?"

———•———

Nathaniel has called just now. It turns out that he did get time off from work and can come home for his brother's birthday, making the drive from Virginia for the celebratory supper. Unusually vague, he hinted about another surprise as well. We will have to wait and see. It is shaping up to be a big weekend for our family.

On the phone with Nathaniel, Bonnie is over the moon with delight. As she twirls the phone cord around her finger and chats excitedly, I have sat down at my desk to remember our firstborn. So much of prayer is a calling to mind.

About halfway through the first year of his life, Nathaniel sat happily next to me while I attempted to compose a prayer for the first chapel service I ever led, which was also the inaugural year of worship in the brand new Bahnson Center at Moravian Seminary. I wanted each word perfect. The afternoon sunlight fell in slants through the window behind Nathaniel's little head, lighting up his red hair and illuminating my silver pen, my special prayer writing pen, which I had laid down momentarily in order to think. My boy seized the opportunity to grab the writing utensil and stuff it in his mouth.

Pleasantly distracted from my task, I smiled at him. Nathaniel thrust his newfound treasure toward my mouth with both hands. Those baby fat arms. I mimicked eating with an extravagant "yum, yum, *yum*" of appreciation. His wide grin displayed all six of his teeth.

Suddenly, there was a whirl, whirl, whirl in the kitchen. Bonnie's mom was visiting from South Carolina for the first time and Grandmother Lois was making her specialty chocolate brownies. Her recipe required a blender, which was a rare sound in our household sure to attract the attention of the curious and innocent.

Temporarily abandoning my efforts to compose the prayer, I carried Nathaniel into the next room, where he could examine said proceedings in that serious way of little people. Lois, whose face shone in the same angled light, offered her only grandson the wooden spoon used to remove the batter from the blades of the blender. The spoon promptly went into his mouth. His eyes shot wide open in amazement. He pulled the spoon back out and there was a half-a-breath pause, a slight deliberation. Only this time, instead of making an offering to his dad, the spoon returned from whence it came. As he continued to slurp away at the tasty combination of sugar, butter, and flour, Grandmother kissed his cheek.

"Smart boy! He knows what he wants."

Bonnie's voice carries into my office.

"Nathaniel, I'm quite sure you will make up your own mind."

She is now laughing at his response. I do not know the subject of their conversation, but this exchange is archetypal of his will and her faith.

While wrapping up a routine trip to the grocery store, I informed the boys that each could select one treat from the rows of candies stacked on either side of the checkout line. Nathaniel immediately chose Skittles. Philip hemmed and hawed, picking up one package and putting it back, weighing his options. He finally decided on peanut M&Ms, which prompted his brother to reply, "I'll allow that."

The elder could be a dictator but, as Bonnie often said, at least he was benevolent.

I was not naïve when Nathaniel left for college. When I was in school, getting drunk on the weekends was the rule. Perhaps if you drank excessively on certain weekdays, then there would be a raised eyebrow. But inebriation was completely normal, even expected. The level of social acceptance is reflected in the number of idioms for intoxication: wasted, blasted, shit-faced, sloppy, throwing back, slamming down, getting lit, torn up, hammered . . . legend holds that Eskimos have over seventy words for snow.

My firstborn, however, has dealt with the demons of prescription drugs, particularly Ritalin. This is commonly prescribed to people with Attention Deficit Disorder. Nathaniel does not have such a diagnosis; his ability to focus is undoubtedly one of his strengths. But he felt tremendous pressure to demonstrate the same high level of academic proficiency he had achieved in high school and, admittedly, much of this strain came from me. I would have much preferred he stay in Pennsylvania and attend one of our excellent state schools. Not only would he have been closer to home, the tuition would have been affordable (if there is such a thing in this age of rising costs). Nathaniel had other ideas. He knew what he wanted and he wanted to attend William and Mary—a fine university, which happens to be one of the priciest in the country. He did receive a nice academic scholarship. But the money came with strings attached, a minimum 3.5 grade point average.

Nathaniel began purchasing Ritalin from friends in order to stay awake and study. Then, he crushed up the pills and snorted the drug so that he could party all night. It was a vicious cycle. He wanted to impress both professors and peers, achieving success and appearing cool. These twin engines fueled his spiral out of control. After a week of heavy drug abuse during spring midterm exams, Nathaniel woke up with a pounding headache and saw blood on his pillow. Thank God that scared him.

Our son had already begun a twelve-step program on his own initiative when he confessed his drug abuse. My reaction was immediate and knee-jerk: Come home! Now! Nathaniel was unwavering in his resolve.

"Dad, I need to prove to myself that I can graduate from this school. I need to do this for me. I am staying."

One of the twelve steps involves undertaking a searching and fearless moral inventory. He can be repaired, Bonnie has constantly reminded me. Something greater is working to mend his broken spirit, restoring our son like a damaged book receives a new spine.

McPherson was also a Godsend to me during this time. We drank countless cups of coffee together, many of mine watered down with tears. He resisted the urge to shush me or say something false meant to be reassuring. As much as I enjoy our lively banter, McPherson is my best friend because he knows when to listen.

I told McPherson how I use to tiptoe quietly to Nathaniel's nursery and crack the door so that a narrow stream of light fell unnoticed upon my sleeping son in the crib. Reassured that he was safe, I would then be able to sleep. And I recalled that, shortly after Philip had been born, Nathaniel began to do exactly what he knew was forbidden, such as attempting to climb the television set. One afternoon, while engaged in this particular stunt, I watched Bonnie scoop him into her strong arms. When he began to wail, she firmly held Nathaniel two inches from her face and declared, "I will keep you safe!" Our boy then rested his head on her collarbone. But he left for college and we could no longer protect him. As McPherson put it late one evening, "There is not even the illusion of control. So maybe there is the opportunity for faith."

God knows I have clung to those words, especially when the times have been dark. Even now, there is something that remains unsettling about my son's experience. I believe Nathaniel is clean, as he says. But I am haunted by how easily he masked portions of his life and presented whatever face would please the people looking at him, including me. I worry that he is hiding something else. Do I truly know my own son, the flesh of my flesh, bone of my bones? O Lord, I believe; help my unbelief!

I do not know where or when she first heard it, but Bonnie has adopted a mantra that it is holy to know what you want. I know that it is now time for bed. And that, first, she and I will pray together.

August 15th, 2000

The phone rang at 4:22 this morning. I incorporated the intrusive sound into my dream as the school bell summoning me to class. I still have the recurring nightmare that I have forgotten to prepare for a test; or, even worse, that I have somehow managed to miss an entire semester and now the final exam looms in front of me on the desk and my entire future hinges on this score. I believe psychologists refer to such dreams as performance anxiety.

Bonnie brought me back to reality.

"The phone," she mumbled.

I offered a weak hello into the receiver. It turns out I was, in fact, being summoned.

"He's gone. Ralph's gone!"

What can you do? You can stumble out of bed, knock around in the bathroom, brush your teeth. You can run a wet comb through what is left your hair and you can pause momentarily before your spouse for a quick kiss, while hastily buttoning your shirt. You can stumble into the kitchen, wonder if there is time for coffee, and decide against it. You can then slip into the night. This is all you can do. You can go.

There were no stars, not even the moon was visible. Cranking the ignition, I thought the engine was chanting a mantra: Ralph. *Helen*. Helen. *Ralph*.

As I drove, I remembered I had seen them in church only this past Sunday. I had noticed how they ate together during Communion. After the service, he had taken my hand, weakly. She had supported him by his arm. Brother Ralph—what had you mentioned in that pause at the door before walking out of my life forever? Those were your last words to me. I hit the steering wheel in frustration. Even now writing at my desk, I have no idea. What did you say?

The rest of our town was asleep, not a single light in any window. I drove down Main Street and turned onto the two-lane highway. The car hummed a new mantra: Death. *Regret.* Regret. *Death.*

The Jibsens lived in one of the oldest neighborhoods in the community, right along the road. I soon pulled into their driveway and saw the modest one-story brick ranch with which I had become intimately familiar. Over these past few months, I visited the Jibsens more often than I had in all the previous years combined. What can you do? You can go to those who are sick and struggling, dying and hoping—hoping against hope. You can try not to live with regrets or nightmares. You can try and pay attention during your waking hours.

As always, I entered through the side door without knocking. There was Sister Helen. But she was as never before, her grief dark under her eyes as she wept at their kitchen table. She rose and knocked her chair backward onto the floor with a loud clatter. Through the blinds, I saw the red flashing lights of the EMT.

I drove home as most of the town was heading to work. People returned my wave with a look of curiosity, which I caught in the fleeting moment through my car windshield. They were imagining what this preacher was doing out so early. I knew they would learn soon enough, likely before lunchtime.

Bonnie was waiting in our kitchen with coffee—bless her. She was dressed for work and, typically, would have already passed through our door. She liked to open the library early for the kids who hung out before class, either reading or listening to their Walkmans at the long oak tables. Would they find what they were searching for among the stacks of books in the early morning hours? The library would be waiting for them regardless. Bonnie, bless her.

She gave the gift of her precious attention to me. Her smile across her coffee cup. *Go on*, her eyes said. *What happened?* She twirled a strand of her dark hair around her finger, head cocked slightly to the side. When I told her about the scene in the Jibsen kitchen, Bonnie put her free hand over her heart. She tapped twice—*He-len*. One of the EMT boys was Jonathan whom she knew from years ago when he hung out in the library before school. I told her how he went straight to the refrigerator door, like he was supposed to do, and saw the Do Not Resuscitate order.

After this last round of chemotherapy had not made a dent in his cancer, Ralph became adamant about his wishes.

"When the Lord's ready, I'm ready!"

He had declared such sentiment several times in my presence, which always prompted his wife to look at the floor, her lips pursed. I was not at all surprised that she had called the ambulance, but I do not judge either. A living will seems like such a logical document, its black letters typed neatly on a white page. But death is not something to wrap your mind around. When it does happen, all we can do is be gentle with one another.

Bonnie uncrossed her legs, getting ready to stand. I stretched my hand across the table, palm open, by which I meant *could you stay for just a few more minutes?* She smiled and sang for me. *One more cup of coffee 'fo I go to the valley below.* One of Mr. Dylan's finest tunes that sounds best coming from her.

———

I crashed on the bed after Bonnie left and remained there until lunchtime, at which point I headed to Evy's for a meal with a side of gossip. I figured I might as well fill in the concerned citizens about the latest news and give them the chance to hear the words straight from my mouth, rather than from hearsay.

Parking my car, I saw Frank Powers cross the road and I headed toward him. My friend shoulders the burden of Parkinson's with more dignity than I can possibly imagine. But it was well past noon and he was "gettin' hangry," meaning a primal anger that came on with a beastly hunger. The brave man was not his best self; normally he would not have tried to kick that mangy feline as it was crossing the street. But his right leg went flying through the air, completely missing the dodgy stray, and spinning him half-way around, causing him to lose his balance and land with a hard thud on the Main Street asphalt. Only after letting fly with a stream of epithets artfully arranged in various and sundry combinations, did he notice his pastor standing three feet away. I inquired into the status of his health.

"Yeah, Wheeler, yeah. Don't you worry about me. Forgive my French there, will you?"

While attempting to help him to his feet, I pulled a little too aggressively. My right foot slipped and we both tumbled backwards. It was the pastor's turn to curse, which Frank Powers took delight in relaying to the usual crowd at Evy's. As I ducked hastily into our usual booth across from McPherson, I could feel the amusement at my expense radiating in the air.

Our conversation turned serious, if only briefly, as I filled in my friend regarding the death. Soon though, we fell into our usual banter about baseball. The Pirates are awful this year, damn it.

Evy brought our food herself, as the proprietor of this establishment often does for her regulars. Unceremoniously, she slid our plates in front of us. "Be sure to pray before you eat, especially for control of the tongue, eh?"

McPherson chuckled. "Ah, yes! It is capable of setting the world on fire, which, unless I am mistaken, is how the *Epistle of James* commonly puts it. Obviously, this James should clearly take such admonishment under prayerful consideration. Or, do you even read the Bible anymore, Wheeler?"

What a smart ass Presbyterian.

Exiting the diner after lunch, I stepped through the door and, once again, was down on my backside. Temporarily blinded by the bright sun, I thought for a moment I had run smack into a brick wall. Actually it was Brandon MacMillan—once one of my skinniest confirmation students, now a man well over six feet tall and three hundred pounds. Everyone calls him Little Mac, of course.

Little Mac kindly helped me back up, wearing his usual lopsided grin. As a boy, he would hold his grandmother's shaky hand, steadying her as they slowly made their way down the aisle to their customary pew near the front of the sanctuary. There was a time when he never missed a Sunday, including the snow days when he was among the faithful and crazy dozen who had managed to dig out their cars and slip-slide to the sanctuary. But as an adult, he had not been to a service in years. Little Mac smiled and nodded in response to my invitation to attend this Sunday's service. We both knew there was a far better chance of running into each other at the diner.

Little Mac's story represents a dramatic change over the course of my relatively short career in ministry. It used to be that boys and girls would grow up in the pew, their legs dangling until they grew tall enough to keep their feet planted firmly on the floor, after which they would get married and then sit beside their own children, whose little legs would hang off the same pews. Now they go off to college and the few who return to town do not come back to church. I am not entirely sure of the reasons for this. It is complicated and seems to grow more confusing every year. I know there are a lot of expert opinions having to do with generational differences and demographic shifts. Sometimes the church is depicted as an innocent bystander, other times as the culprit. But the undeniable fact is that a generation is missing. Equally evident is that our communities are suffering as a result.

I have been around long enough to remember when young adult men were active members. Steve Lewis was an electrician by trade and all-around handyman by God-given ability. Before Ben and Michael were born, even before his wife, Betsy, was in the picture, my friend would spend most Saturday mornings assisting the elderly with any number of odd jobs. He invited me to come along and install the first clothes dryer that ever graced Gertrude Burke's home. Wanting to feel useful, I offered to help with the wiring and Steve agreed, knowing that I most likely had not learned such things in seminary. When I finished, he flipped on the machine and immediately received the buzz of a sharp electric shock. Steve only laughed and said that he could now tell his Pentecostal cousin that he, too, had felt the Holy Ghost.

Until he left for college, Little Mac allowed the younger boys to trail behind him down to the pond most Sunday evenings. I started fishing with my sons only when they could no longer follow their hero.

Little Mac seems to be doing well. His grandmother updates me every couple of months from her room at Pleasant Shade. He has a good job, just bought a larger house, and plans to marry on a beach somewhere down south. I wish him the best and, of course, offer my prayers.

I watched this gentle giant throw his hand out of the truck window as he pulled away, greeting Sister Patsy Miller. This diminutive matriarch of our church used to teach all the boys and girls in children's Sunday school. She sent them to the youth class when they grew taller than her. It was just as much a rite of passage as taking the first Communion.

"Sure would be nice to see him in church," she said wistfully.

I had agreed with her, but this is not quite the right word. "Nice" cannot shoulder the blessed burden of the holy calling to nurture God's children throughout their entire lives. I think of my boys. It would be nice if they would come back and stay longer than a weekend. But what will happen to the next generation? What about Charlie and Ben and Michael? Who will allow them to tag along on those countless journeys in which boys sprint ahead, trip and skin their knees, only to stagger back up and stumble once more toward becoming men?

I spent the remainder of the afternoon buying a new suit. This chore was long overdue, as my primary Sunday outfits have been looking decidedly below their best. And they are decidedly too snug. This is the reason why I dread going.

Dad took every opportunity to shame me about my appearance. He was a three sport athlete in high school and could never understand why I was not. I can still hear him. *Are you really going to sit around all day with your nose in some book?* After Mom died, I had no one to stick up for me. I would reach for seconds. *Haven't you had enough to eat?* That only made me want to eat more.

I try to exercise and eat well. In recent years, I have spent far more time here at this desk working out my problems than actually working out. Though my arms and legs are somewhat skinny, my belly is pudgy over my belt. I have showcased an extra chin for years and seem to be auditioning for a third. Thank God there is not a retailer in town. I have to get on the interstate and drive over twenty miles to a place where, unlike Evy's, nobody would think twice if I cursed.

The young salesman could have doubled as James Bond in his tuxedo. This was not even a particularly high-end store. How do the beautiful people live? They must have their own set of regrets, but damn, it would seem nice for a change. As James Bond took my measurements, he offered some suggestions regarding my wardrobe. I shook him off. No amount of cuffing or creasing or any expense could make me look any less dumpy and roly-poly. No sense trying to pretend otherwise. The truth will set you free, but not until it has finished roughing you up.

On the way out of the store, a young man stopped me.

"Aren't you the pastor at Talmage Moravian?"

Philip taught me a phrase a few years ago: Too Much Information. He claimed that T.M.I. is the number one occupational hazard for parish ministers. He is a preacher's kid, after all. He has witnessed complete strangers spill their most intimate details in public places.

So I nodded hesitantly, unsure as to whether this might be one of those awkward interruptions that, if not painfully uncomfortable, would at least delay my return to town. But this young man was no stranger. He was the great-nephew of Peter Davidson, the man everyone knew as Buster. This name jogged my memory and I recognized him as that handsome kid from the City, studying at NYU to be a lawyer, right? No, he corrected me, it was finance; but, yes, he had flown in for the graveside service years ago in God's Acre. Now he lives in Brooklyn and is back for a quick visit, just happened to need a few new ties and, wow, the prices sure are cheaper down here!

"But, Pastor, I'm glad I've run into you after all these years. I still remember my great uncle's service. And I want you to know that funeral was beautiful. The most beautiful ever."

Now that comment made my chest puff out a little, perhaps even a little further than my belly.

—⋅—

There is only one person in this year's confirmation class. Charlie was pleasant enough, if rather tight-lipped at first, as is the way of most adolescent boys. But when you talk every other Tuesday evening for several months, formalities fade, trust develops, confession ensues. Now I never know where he is headed in our rambling conversations until we have arrived.

Charlie is twelve years old, going on thirteen. He typically rides his BMX across his stepfather's farm, zooming over the bridge and the rushing creek below, careening recklessly onto the blacktop road as he boasts he will when he can finally drive a car. Charlie is twelve years old and already dreaming of sixteen.

At his best friend's house, he is the tallest and strongest among the half-dozen boys. And everyone knows it. He throws every ball as hard as he can. Sometimes his friends duck out of the way rather than attempt a catch. His best friend recently dyed purple streaks in his hair and a well-aimed football once rocketed off his multicolored head. Everyone laughed, including Charlie. While the other boys were chasing down the wayward ball, he checked on his best friend to make sure he was okay. All the boys ignore the three kid sisters playing on the swing set.

These adolescents grow tired of sports in the backyard, and Charlie often leads them back to his stepfather's farm where he tries his best to entertain them. It seems that his pack is always in search of something new. They want to do something exhilarating! They no longer climb trees, although Charlie had loved to ascend the large maples only a year ago. They never wander inside where parents might lurk. They love to curse.

Over the past weekend, Charlie marched his friends out to the chicken run, moving quickly past the rusted swing set without pausing. Dozens of white hens were clucking around, pecking at dirt for bugs or whatever desire goes through their pea-sized brains. Charlie barely gave them a second glance. He had eyes only for the roosters.

These beasts with shiny black feathers and blood red crowns let fly their full-throated, banshee shrieks as Charlie stepped closer. He calmly watched the largest rooster rake the brown soil with his right claw, its sharp talons spraying dirt. Charlie took off at a dead sprint straight for that bird. The panicked rooster fled in the opposite direction, but to no avail. Mimicking his stepfather, Charlie flipped the bird upside down and held its legs together with one hand. He added his own unique twist, raising his trophy high in the air for all to see, as the irate rooster flapped impotently. His friends had formed a half-circle around him, but quickly backed away when he offered the prize to each one in turn. Charlie's smile was boyish when he told me that.

He began throwing the bird up in the air and catching it on the way back down. At first intuition that he was losing his audience, Charlie spun in a complete circle while the beast was dropping madly through the air, and hauled in the bird just a fraction of a second before it smacked itself silly upon the ground. For his next trick, he attempted a catch behind his back. The rooster hit the ground running, scattering the rest of the boys like they were frightened hens.

Corralling that damn bird once again, Charlie hauled the thing calmly out of the chicken run. His friends followed cautiously at a safe distance. They approached the creek, running low and shallow in the wide bend beyond the house, beyond the view of anyone who might happen to glance out of the window. Near the water, Charlie cried out, "Hut, hut, *hike!*" Cocking the bird dangerously close to his right ear, he launched the feathered beast in a wide arc. The other boys shrieked and the silly creature plopped into the water. As he fished out the rooster, a lightning bolt flashed across Charlie's mind—he could wring the bird's neck with his bare hands. In the retelling of this epic adventure to his pastor, Charlie involuntarily shivered at the thought.

His family lives on a small farm; his stepfather prefers it that way. Charlie has heard him say at least a hundred times in three years that a farmer only needs enough land to watch with his own two eyes. So Charlie knew deep down that he had been seen, and he was quiet throughout dinner, waiting for the other shoe to drop. His stepfather broached the subject of the rooster's near-lynching only after his mom and little sisters had left to clean the dishes.

Charlie confessed. He knew what he had done was wrong; he could not say exactly why he did it.

Predictably, the punishment was stern. No television for a week. But his stepfather offered his hand when he got up to leave. And Charlie took it, squeezing for all he was worth . . . like men do, right Pastor?

Yes, the ties that bind are mysterious. When I was his age, I always kissed Mom goodnight on the lips. I shared that with Charlie and he just nodded.

———————

The weather this afternoon was bright and beautiful, perfect for running errands with the windows down. It was also a sad day with some strangely wonderful moments and some wonderfully strange ones, too. And I was busy. I did not have the chance to pray through my daily devotion until just now, right before bed.

The Moravian Church publishes the Daily Texts for every day of the year, each reading comprised of selected verses from both the Old and New Testaments, along with stanzas from usually two different hymns as accompaniment to the scriptures. The assigned passages are known as watchwords. This devotional practice is traced all the way back to our Z-man who gave the congregation at Herrnhut a "Losung" at the end of every evening, which was intended to guide and nurture throughout the following day. The Bible verses were drawn by lot, though I would not say they were randomly selected. The practice of a chance drawing professes reliance upon the inspiration of the Holy Spirit.

Many people at Talmage Moravian are more faithful to this daily discipline. But the devotion book also offers specific prayers for different groups of people on each day of the week. Tuesdays include intercession for those young people enrolled in colleges and universities. Maybe I am not as faithful as I should be, but I never fail to pray.

As I closed my prayer tonight, an image of Philip came to mind from around the time he was three. He strolled into my study, clasped the Daily Texts, pressed the book to his dear little heart and sighed.

"I *love* this book, Daddy."

Those green eyes—there are moments when he looks so much like his mother.

Perhaps it was inevitable that our youngest would rebel. In high school, he was compared constantly to Nathaniel. His older brother was an excellent student and never in trouble. And then there was his preacher father. Jesus told a famous parable about fathers and sons. In asking for his share of the inheritance, the younger son, known as the prodigal, was essentially informing Dad that he wished him dead. I never imagine that Philip went that far, but he clearly wanted some separation.

Over spring break his freshman year of college, Philip pulled into our driveway, squeezing in a visit with his parents before heading back to Penn State in the morning. This planned stop was on the heels of his first adventure to New York City. What was not discussed ahead of time was the young woman who got out of the car with him. Her revealing top and tight mini-skirt did not make the best first impression. Still, we managed dinner pleasantly enough. Afterward Bonnie told our guest that she could sleep in Nathaniel's vacant room. Philip informed his mother that, no, she would be sleeping in his room. I forget how he put it exactly. I will never forget how my son glared at me as he spoke. Those green eyes!

Another tradition developed regarding the watchwords. A person, generally the pastor, would prayerfully select a specific verse for an important and holy occasion such as a wedding or ordination. I have chosen watchwords for each student who has gone through confirmation. During the service, I place my hand on each child's forehead and recite the verse from memory. I have now forgotten most of them. But Philip's was 1 John 4:12: *No one has ever seen God, but if we love one another, God lives in union with us, and his love is made perfect in us.*

This is the Good News Translation, which remains the Bible version our church presents to each confirmand. But even as I recited the verse over my son's head, I was troubled by one specific word. "Perfect" is not quite the right word for a young person to hear. Though I am not a scholar of New Testament Greek, I know enough to understand that the original meaning has nothing to do with moral perfection as in sinlessness; the term implies a sense of wholeness, completeness, maturity. I said as much to my son, but maybe the last thing he needed to think was that I expected him to be perfect.

I was hard on him, especially when he was a teenager. Nathaniel, as stubborn as he was, was still more of a pleaser. I guess it fell to Philip to play the role of button pusher. Our fights would typically begin over something inconsequential that, for some reason, I had decided was absolutely essential. The new jeans he had intentionally ripped at the knees. Those flannel shirts he would only wear if they were three sizes too big. The chain attached to his wallet that hung down from his pants, never failing to remind me of prison shackles. He was trying on a self far different from his father. I understand that now. Why did I struggle to view him through a lens of grace? It is hard to have self-awareness when there are two teenagers in your house, especially if you are not particularly self-confident.

After a nasty shouting match one evening, I stomped into his room because I had thought of some final retort. I forget exactly what I had intended to say. God only knows the reason we were at each other's throats in the first place. As soon as he spied me standing in his bedroom doorway, Philip sprang to his feet as if catapulted. He was twelve years old, going on thirteen, and already taller than me. Looking at him, the urge to fight drained away like dirty water rushing down the pipes.

I managed to mumble some vague apology, which likely sounded half-hearted at best. I could not even meet his eyes. I had a sudden revelation—*maybe if I just hold you.* So I took tentative steps across the room, a prodigal father, and tried to embrace my youngest son. Philip's left arm draped over my shoulder and down my back; but the open palm of his right hand lay flat against my chest. He both squeezed me close and pushed me away. I have prayed about this perfect lesson ever since, often on Tuesdays when I pray for those young people enrolled in colleges and universities.

August 16th, 2000

I know without looking that Bonnie is fixing pancakes for breakfast.

Today is the sixteenth of August.

Bonnie confronts life. She has taught me that marriage is a wrestling of the ego, a giving of self by altogether selfish people. Through this holy struggle, relationships are rebuilt and people are redeemed. Like Jacob striving all night against the angel, she lives as though the blessing is only possible through the pain. The blessing limps forward.

"Jaime, my love, everything's ready."

The sixteenth of August.

Today is just another Wednesday for most people. I must select the hymns for Sunday. This is actually a welcome distraction, though picking music is more contentious than ever before in my career. We now have something called "worship wars"—there is a contradiction in terms.

McPherson learned about a recent survey among Presbyterians, which asked the faithful across the country to select their most beloved hymn and, alternatively, their least favorite. Wouldn't you know it, the exact same song was at the top of both lists: "How Great Thou Art." The battle lines are drawn. But though the adult choir is often identified as the War Department of the church, experience teaches that youth fight hardest against change.

It was 1982, my first summer as pastor, and the adult leadership had decided to change the closing hymn at the end of summer camp. "Kumbaya" was the long-running tradition, yet they substituted a song entitled "Sanctuary" that had been published that year. I assume they intended to update the spiritual experience in order to reach a new generation. What followed was an actual revolt. Instead of the newly assigned song, a group of students began to sing the old familiar and the swelling of youth voices eventually drowned out the worship leaders on stage. To hell with the new.

I was already familiar with the rituals at Camp Laurel Ridge. During our first full year of marriage, the two of us spent the summer of 1973 there in the mountains of North Carolina. I worked as a college counselor and it was a good gig. We were the only married couple among the summer staff, so we had a little cabin all to ourselves. A creek bubbled outside the back door. A choir of birds praised in the trees above. Flowers in Bonnie's hair, flowers everywhere. Life was like a folk song. In the evenings, I ambled down to the campfire and picked a few tunes on my secondhand guitar. Though I was teaching myself to play, people were gracious and sang along—sometimes loudly to cover my mistakes.

I was sliding the guitar back into its case when a sixth grader sidled up to me. He was rail thin with a protruding pimpled nose and blond hair hanging over his eyes, which gave him the appearance of an upright mop. Awkwardly brushing back his shaggy strands, he mumbled some vague desire to learn how to play. The last thing I wanted was an added commitment. But the boy looked so hopeful. How hard could it be?

Word soon spread and five students tromped through the door the next afternoon, each sporting the same moppy hairstyle. Those boys offered their jittery salutations in a voice-cracking chorus and sank into the beat up couches in the corner of the large recreation room, each balancing an electric guitar across his knees, instruments which looked brand new from the gleam of the strings. How they had managed to convince their parents to transport such guitars to a rustic mountain camp was beyond me. But visible even behind all that hair was a shining hope in their eyes. What did these mop-heads expect from me, some kind of miracle?

I suggested we begin by learning to tune their instruments. Ninety painful minutes later, we were still hard at work on that basic first step. I tromped into the cabin and informed Bonnie that my career as a guitar teacher was over. She pried her eyes from her tattered copy of *Jane Eyre*.

"Jaime, they just might surprise you."

Those boys kept showing up, despite the fact they were decidedly uninterested in learning anything I actually knew how to play like "Tangled Up in Blue" or "Shelter in the Storm" or "Amazing Grace" for that matter. They only wanted to rock out, but Jimi Hendrix riffs were far above and beyond my limited abilities. Still, on every Wednesday for the rest of that summer, they would trek to practice, guitars slung over their skinny shoulders, when they could have been swimming or shooting hoops or goggling the older girls in camp like the rest of their peers. I realize now they were teaching me how coaxing the perfect riff from six stubborn strings is actually something like faith.

We did have one public performance. The final Sunday morning of the summer entailed a closing worship service for all in attendance, including parents who had arrived to collect their offspring. Before the "Kumbaya" chorus marked the close of our time together, five campers clustered on the camp stage, each with his electric guitar, each looking to rock out Jesus-style, each with long hair over his eyes. Bonnie had dubbed their band By Faith, Not Sight. Hoping they could nonetheless perceive my instructions, I prompted this unlikely ensemble to start more or less on time, just as we had practiced. Their guitars were not even in tune. But those boys grinned from ear to ear.

Not only can I call to mind their smiling faces, I can still manage some of the melodies from my one and only guitar class, including the opening riff of "Purple Haze" that we learned together that summer. When Nathaniel and Philip were toddlers, I often strummed through one of the old familiars to entertain them. My boys beamed widely from the moment I pulled my old guitar out of its case, their eyes sparkling from behind their mops. Bonnie has always liked long-haired boys.

Spent some time today on the upcoming funeral service. I have attended many such ceremonies in various churches over the years and people tend to say the same things regardless of denomination. We stand around, snacking at the reception, and someone will bring up how the deceased never harmed nobody, which will prompt another to note how that person never had an unkind word to say. Right down to the fizzy nonalcoholic punch, this scene will be reenacted after Brother Ralph's service. I do not have to plan that.

But we Moravians have a distinctive history. From the beginning, the brothers and sisters were avid writers and faithful keepers of diaries. Each member of a Moravian congregation was also charged with composing a kind of memoir called a *lebenslauf*. Thoreau claimed to write "a meteorological journal of the mind," which compares favorably to my way of thinking. But most Moravians offer a spiritual autobiography in which the major personal events are considered in relationship to God. Roughly translated, *lebenslauf* means "course of life" but the text often reads as if someone was composing his or her own funeral homily. I marvel at such courage.

I am reliant upon translations of the early *lebenslaufs*—often rendered in Victorian prose. It is humorous that Modern Moravians are still influenced by the form.

I, Ralph Davis Jibsen IV, was born on the twelve of May in the year of Our Lord 1932.

This made me chuckle for other reasons as well. He was the only fourth I have ever known, yet he was known as "Junior" to his three older sisters.

Like the removal of a fancy overcoat, a modern *lebenslauf* abandons such formality quickly. The writing kicks off its shoes and becomes comfortable, even intimate. In most cases, family and friends will read the manuscript only after the author has died. Yet the power of crafting and shaping a personal testimony can shape one's own sense of who he or she is today. Writing can be a form of therapy. Like any counseling technique, the key is courageous vulnerability.

Brother Ralph notes his marriage, recording the day and place and time. He adds that they did not have any children.

There will never be a Ralph Davis Jibsen V, but I trust this was the Lord's will.

How brave that sentence is.

He left it at that, going on to talk about his professional career and service to Talmage Moravian. There is more ink devoted to his championing of the sanctuary's new roof than anything else. During these last months, I had encouraged him to write; but I saw this morning that the last event he recorded was his retirement party almost two years ago. Absolutely no mention of his cancer.

The task to finish the *lebenslauf* falls to the pastor. I typically return to the formal tone.

Brother Ralph Jibsen went to be with God on the morning of the fifteenth of August in the year of Our Lord 2000, passing away gently and blessedly, joining his parents and three sisters in the light perpetual and the glory everlasting.

Lovely, I think. Such formality serves as a kind of Sunday best. I never want to air anyone's dirty laundry.

But Sister Helen Jibsen did confide in me once. *Mis*-carriage, she had carefully enunciated. Lots of words start with the same prefix, she had noted. By way of studied observation, she ticked them off on the fingers of one hand: Mismanaged. Misplaced. Misstep. Misunderstanding. Mistrust.

"And not one of them positive, eh, Reverend Wheeler?"

Mis-*carriage*, she continued. When she was a little girl, she had loved carriages. Cinderella rode in one, remember? Oh, how she would linger on that bright colorful page of her story book, tracing the carriage's golden wheels with her finger, carefully moving up and down each spoke. She never wanted to flip the page to the mean sisters. The story stopped when Cinderella first entered the carriage. It never turned back into a pumpkin.

Her husband did not speak about such things, not even to his wife. He certainly did not say the word *miscarriage* to his pastor. But I did learn of a certain neighborhood child who came into this world with a hole in his heart. This family already boasted a dozen or more kids, so there was not much time afforded to this little one with special needs. For three evenings a week, over the course of several years, Ralph Davis Jibsen IV would walk to this child's home immediately after work. He taught the boy to read and write, mostly by way of the Bible. This was before my time at Talmage, but under my hand, this will go in his *lebenslauf*. So will this:

I once challenged the congregation with a pointed question at the end of a sermon. Brother Ralph Jibsen was one of the first people to meet me at the door after the benediction, which was unusual, for he generally stayed behind to straighten up the sanctuary, putting away the bulletins and whatnot. He was never much for socializing, including the post-postlude chit-chat. But that Sunday, there he was.

"Reverend Wheeler, you asked what difference our faith makes in our lives, right? I'll tell you. This is what I say. God gives us a heart big enough to tuck people inside."

Such words of courageous vulnerability should be preserved.

Funeral preparations or not, the sixteenth of August is a day for reflection. It helps to write.

"Guitar" was one of the first words Nathaniel ever pronounced, but he only learned to play during his junior year of college. I remain grateful for this, although his intensity toward the craft of songwriting has proven to be a detriment to his grades. It will likely take an extra semester or two for Nathaniel to graduate. So be it. It is holy to know what you want.

By his senior year, our son had started a band called The Midgets, largely because his mandolin player was six feet, eight inches tall. The flair for names comes honestly by his mother. That fall, Bonnie and I saw The Midgets compete in a battle of the bands held on the campus quad. They finished in second place after the debut of a song "Words," which Nathaniel had written. The lyrics involve certain terms that double as both nouns and verbs, which proved once and for all that he is the son of a librarian.

Red is a color you can see if you look; and read's what you done when you've finished the book; a perch is a fish that swims in the sea; and if you're cute you can perch right next to me.

There were only three bands in that competition.

His mother sings these lyrics while puttering around the house, smiling to herself, as she did this morning after pancakes. When he last visited over Easter, Nathaniel surprised us by performing songs from *Blood on the Tracks*, accompanying himself with one of those harmonica holders like Mr. Dylan. That's our boy.

The times they are a-changin' and, these days, the majority of Nathaniel's playing is in service to a non-denominational, non-traditional worship gathering geared toward evangelizing high school students. They pointedly do not refer to themselves as a church. Still, I could not help but wonder out loud about a career in ministry. I reminded Nathaniel that his father had started out playing guitar around a campfire. If history does not repeat itself, then it often rhymes. We will have to wait and see.

Came home from lunch and found Bonnie sitting with Betsy Lewis for their monthly tea. Betsy is the perfect conversation partner for my wife, sharing a love of nineteenth-century romantic literature and twenty-first-century liberal politics. They extol the Bronte sisters and bash Newt Gingrich on a regular basis. But not today.

Puffy red eyes and a small mountain of crumpled tissues meant they had been discussing the Bad Thing. Separated by a span of fifteen years and the distance from South Carolina to Pennsylvania, their stories are nonetheless strikingly similar. Heart-wrenchingly so. How the pain woke them up screaming. How there was so much blood. How they were rushed to the emergency room although everyone, including them, knew there was nothing to be done. I knew all those details. Betsy shared something new today.

After her Bad Thing, Betsy had held her daughter—cupped her, more precisely, for the baby was no bigger than the palm of her mother's small hand. Betsy's daughter was dead; she understood that.

"But there was a shimmer around her," Betsy whispered. "You know?"

Bonnie nodded.

Dabbing her eyes with a fresh tissue, Betsy described a single strand of auburn hair, gracefully curled in the middle of the baby's forehead. Gazing tearfully upon that tiny wisp accented against the backdrop of pale skin, she was reminded of an apostrophe of possession.

"She will always be *my* child."

I squeezed Bonnie's hand twice—our child.

In today's mail, I found a flyer advertising our alma mater's Homecoming. There was Bonnie's smiling face among the old photographs. That is good promotion work.

Lenoir-Rhyne College, in the year of Our Lord 1971, first day of orientation. Freshmen were instructed to toss their newly-issued IDs into one of three large boxes in the center of the Shuford Gym. A couple of upperclassmen leaders shook them up and invited us to select one of the cards at random. We had to match the photo on the card to the face in real life.

I drew Bonnie's.

My spiritual autobiography must include how the course of my life was forever impacted by a chance drawing. Or, like the early Moravians and their watchwords, could I claim this was the work of the Holy Spirit?

Bonnie had selected another young woman's ID and found her easily. She was standing alone by the bleachers, watching our classmates with a bemused smile on her face—always has been a keen observer of the human condition. Her eyes were greener and brighter in person than on the card. To this day, photos do not do her justice.

We sat on the bleachers, inching closer and closer, flirting and laughing until they sent everyone back to the separate dorms. Sexual revolution or not, there were certain appearances to maintain. Our alma mater is historically affiliated with the Lutheran Church. We met for lunch in the cafeteria the next day and were nearly inseparable thereafter. It was a whirlwind, the very best kind. We were caught up in the wild intoxicating Now of young love, which became stronger and more addicting each day. I went home to meet her parents over winter break, my first trip to South Carolina. We made love for the first time there. In her father's basement. When her parents were at church. On Christmas Eve. Sin boldly, said Martin Luther.

On the last day of classes for the spring semester, I met her on those bleachers in the gym. It was sweltering hot, but Bonnie had insisted on meeting in our old spot because she had something to tell me.

"I am pregnant. You, James Wheeler, will marry me."

Bonnie confronts life.

Her daddy was a Free Will Baptist. Even after we were married, he insisted that I address him as Mr. Jackson. He held rigid absolutes about right and wrong, which he had sought to impose upon his only child. He clearly did not approve of his daughter having free will. Our youngest son has come by his rebellious streak honestly, an irony not lost upon me.

When Bonnie and I returned from a honeymoon at Myrtle Beach that had been tragically cut short, we sat at her childhood kitchen table and she tearfully confessed the Bad Thing. Her mama had fixed pancakes for supper. Pancakes. And Mr. Jackson, viciously stabbing one with his fork, quoted a biting scripture: *the wage of sin is death.*

It would be several years before Bonnie spoke to him again. As for me, I started writing a daily journal.

I would not want Mr. Jackson to be remembered in solely negative terms; in fact, I rather came to admire him. In complete contradiction to my father's lack of faith, his unshakable convictions impressed me as a defiant shout above the deafening roar of uncertainty in the universe. But I also believe my desire to please Mr. Jackson was a way to assuage my own guilt. I could never bring our daughter back to life; perhaps I could restore his relationship with his daughter.

I called him long distance at the end of every month for the rest of our undergraduate careers. Our initial conversations were terse, often strained. No longer a blazing fire of fury, his anger had iced into frigid silence. He was locked in a battle of wills with his daughter and the key had been thrown away. But as Bonnie's silence lengthened, he came to hunger for any words about her. I see now that Mr. Jackson was the first person I ever intentionally ministered to.

As for free will and the providence of God, well, the more time passes, the less I know. Saint Paul wrote that we are all working out our salvation with fear and trembling. Mr. Jackson tried to instill fear; maybe he was, in fact, afraid. I interpret Paul to suggest

that the meaning of life is not always clear. Why else would we walk
by faith not sight? Like Brother Ralph Jibsen, I trust the Lord's will.
And it helps to have someone walking beside you. Maybe someone
to share tea or pancakes. The blessing limps forward.

Oak Arnold telephoned after supper. As the head usher, he sought details regarding Friday's funeral arrangements. I would have communicated with him first thing in the morning, but Oak has never been one to wait. A lifelong military man, he retired a couple of years ago and began attending our church at the invitation of Frank Powers, my faithful friend who seems to reach out to every single veteran in the surrounding counties. Oak immediately reminded me of my father-in-law, both in appearance and manner. Not to mention political leanings. Oak would make a good Free Will Baptist proud.

Since arriving at Talmage Moravian, he has sought to impose a regimental discipline upon the congregation. We now have sign-up sheets for all volunteers and Oak constantly reminds us that showing up on time is arriving ten minutes late. Mr. Jackson used to say the same damn thing.

Unlike my father-in-law, Oak had been a wild youth. Sin boldly. He was one to carouse, as he puts it. He grew up in rural West Virginia, the kind of town that had a single stoplight so that drunks would have something to shoot at. One starry night, Oak had already had a few too many when he decided to take his father's car out for a spin. He also deemed it appropriate to take along a six-pack for entertainment purposes. He was zooming down a back road when he finished the last beer and decided to chuck it. The can arced up and over the roof of his car and clanged off top of the sheriff's parked vehicle. This officer had been dozing through his night shift.

"But you best believe he woke up quick," Oak tells it with a laugh.

After a high-speed chase, Oak spent the night in jail and agreed to enlist if all charges were dropped. He is one of those who ardently believe the military is the best thing that can happen to a young man. It made him who he is today and he is convinced that is God's will for his life. Who am I to argue?

We have, however, butted heads on a number of occasions, specifically about certain passages in the Bible. Oak is a "wage-of-sin-is-death" kind of guy and has no problem seeing God's hand in victorious military combat. While there is some Old Testament precedent for this, it is rather hard to square with such teachings as turn the other cheek, pray for those who persecute you, and love your enemies. In terms of my sermons, I have tried to impress upon Oak that his real quarrel is with Jesus, not me. That has not gone over very well.

"Wheeler, you sure are a pain in the ass!"

I told him, no, I was Moravian. Mercifully, he laughed.

Presbyterians have their Calvin and predestination, Methodists their Wesley and sanctification. We Moravians have our Z-man and his "heart religion," which emphasizes personal piety. He came to believe whole-heartedly in the paramount significance of a personal relationship with Jesus Christ. Zinzendorf preached and practiced loving kindness and self-sacrifice. Regardless of doctrinal differences, he argued that we all pray to the same God. We are one family, brothers and sisters. Such theology is nothing new, really; yet it has likely saved my marriage.

After two years of ministry here in this community, it came time for Philip to start kindergarten. In theory, Bonnie could now pursue her dream of returning to school. But a certain director of graduate admissions slowly removed her horn-rimmed spectacles and plopped them unceremoniously upon Bonnie's application. Leaning back in her plush office chair, she addressed my wife across the formidable desk.

"My dear," the director began, before pausing to clear her throat with a dignified cough. "Perhaps you would be best served by considering a different career path."

Bonnie has always loved books. According to her mother, Lois, she pranced to her father's bookshelf, traced her finger down a book, and sounded out each word. Bonnie was four and her perfect pronunciation sent shivers down her mother's spine.

I had heard this story. I had also witnessed my wife's sparkling intellect firsthand. She always made better grades. At Lenoir-Rhyne, the English faculty included a married couple, both of whom encouraged Bonnie to major in British literature. I casually mentioned to these professors one afternoon between classes that

I was considering switching my course of study from History to English as well.

"Oh no," they said in unison. She quickly added, "James, we would not want you to hold back such a promising student."

They should require all faculty members to take a few classes in pastoral care.

After that less than graceful response from the admissions director, I felt the signs were pointing Bonnie in the direction of staying home with our boys. She thought otherwise. During one argument, I emphatically stated that this was God's will for her life.

My God, how could I have said that? I have taken pastoral care!

For a strained period of time, I reminded Bonnie of the worst of her father. All that pain flooded back into our marriage, nearly drowning us.

But there was a group of older women at Talmage Moravian Church. I do not know if these saints knew to quote Zinzendorf and his theories concerning heart religion. I do know they emphatically disagreed with the pastor's assessment of his wife's future. When Bonnie tearfully confessed her rejection to the graduate program in library science, they pledged their unqualified support. One babysat the boys so that she could study and re-take the GRE. Another edited her new application. Still another coerced a friend of a friend on the faculty to write a sterling recommendation. All of these women shared countless cups of tea and, when it was more helpful, a bottle of wine. I think about Sister Wilma and how she claimed to have finished everything she *had* to do about twenty years ago. Those women gave Bonnie the gift of their time. Those sisters in faith helped keep our heads above water.

Many of those women now rest in God's Acre. But they all saw Bonnie graduate at the top of her class from that very same university. How those sisters loved to clear their throats with a dignified cough and ask if perhaps she might be best served by considering a different career path! I am grateful that I could laugh along with them. Unlike my father-in-law, I have learned to admit my mistakes. The Lord's ways are inscrutable. But never doubt Bonnie Jackson Wheeler's holy vision of what she wants.

As I gave Oak Arnold his marching orders for Friday's service, I was reminded of one visit a few years ago. Instead of talking politics and religion, we drank beer and listened to Johnny Cash. After a few records and a few more drinks, Oak told me about the first time he heard the Man in Black. Half-drunk and looking to get all the way there, he had wandered into some bar when, suddenly, this voice came over the jukebox.

"I tell you, Wheeler, music like that hits you in the chest. And it changes you."

I think about that moment when he is a pain in my ass. And I pray that I can continue to change for Bonnie.

———•———

The sixteenth of August and the world spins on. As is true of most churches across the country, Wednesday night means choir practice. So Marjorie Stemlich flies down the back roads a good fifteen, maybe twenty miles over the speed limit. She knows that cops park down by the wide bend of the stream, fishing for traffic violators. But she is always late.

Marjorie's old Chevy squeals to a stop in the parking lot. She hustles up the sidewalk, her arms full of sheet music, which we all hope match the hymns I have selected. Marjorie bursts into the sanctuary and heads straight for the piano, which has been pushed into the right-hand corner. She plops down and scoots toward the keys, as the old wooden bench underneath her protests with crotchety creaks. The choir members all quiet down, for this is their cue. Marjorie is their general.

Her steady hands provide the tunes for our worship service every Sunday. Given that nearly all Moravians love to sing, her leadership is indispensable and invaluable. She plays no extra notes and rarely makes even the slightest mistake. Week in and week out, year after year, she has skillfully provided exactly what we need. And she is a volunteer. I am reminded of a Joni Mitchell song—our pianist *plays real good for free*.

A few months ago during worship, I sat contemplating my closing charge to the congregation when it hit me that Marjorie was playing Leonard Cohen's "Hallelujah" as the offertory. She ably concluded and launched right into the Old One Hundredth doxology. But in that brief pause in between songs, I saw her smile to herself—the secret of quiet laughter.

Most Wednesdays, Marjorie leaves the parking lot as quickly as she arrives. I happen to know that she often pulls over onto the highway shoulder. The old engine gives a hiss when it is cut off, which she prefers to hear as a grateful sigh, for the chance to rest is rare. When the weather is clear, she rolls down her window. Leaning back in her seat, Marjorie closes her eyes and quiets her heart.

As I finish my writing just now, Bonnie steps into my study and asks if she might read what I have written. I will show her the last couple of pages. She loves Marjorie.

"But, Jamie, I thought you'd write about Daddy today."

Mr. Jackson suffered a massive stroke on the thirteenth of August in the year of Our Lord 1978. I was still in seminary, interning for the summer at a church near Old Salem, North Carolina. I had helped serve Holy Communion for the first time. Bonnie and I were actually discussing anniversary plans when the phone rang. She was nine months pregnant. She should not have gone to South Carolina. There was no stopping her.

The air conditioner in our Pontiac was broken. The line of stopped traffic seemed to melt before my eyes in the blurry heat off the asphalt. Nathaniel threw up twice in the back seat. Bonnie had to stop and pee countless times.

Grandmother Lois met us in the parking lot and immediately swooped Nathaniel away to the hospital cafeteria, luring our boy with the promise of ice cream. I am not sure if her brave face was for Nathaniel's sake or Bonnie's. Over her shoulder, she called out the room number on the fifth floor ICU. Naturally, the elevator was out of service. In another time and place, it might have been comical to struggle up those stairs, tired and hot and pregnant.

The sound reached us in the hallway. "Death rattle" is the only way to describe his labored breathing.

We stayed only a couple of hours, mostly listening to the blip of machines hooked to his body. There was no shimmer to him, no holy moment to this Bad Thing. I tried holding a conversation with Bonnie. She was as silent as her father. I mumbled some defeated prayers. Mr. Jackson was completely unresponsive. Bonnie did not cry.

We spent the night in the basement of the Jackson's home. We could have gone upstairs. Except for that quick trip to the cafeteria in deference to Nathaniel, Lois never left his side until he breathed his last. We put Nathaniel to sleep in the trundle bed and collapsed beside him on the old couch. Only then did Bonnie begin to cry. She silently sobbed herself to sleep in a way she had never done before . . . or has ever since.

Brother Philip Jackson went to be with God on the morning of the sixteenth of August in the year of Our Lord 1978. On his tombstone, we had a verse from the Book of Revelation engraved.

Blessed are the dead which die in the Lord henceforth: yea, saith the Spirit, that they may rest from their labors; and their works do follow them.

August 17th, 2000

From time to time a visitor to our cemetery will remark that the deceased are apparently scattered willy-nilly—why aren't husbands and wives buried together? It is true there are no family plots. The dead in God's Acre are buried according to gender and marital status. Married men are in one section, married women in another. Unmarried men and women likewise have separate sections. Such groups are traditionally referred to as "choirs" and there is space reserved for children and infants as well. And our dead are laid to rest chronologically according to the date of their passing.

On this gorgeous morning, I paused to pray at the spot of Betsy's baby. There is a perfect view of the sunrise—a picture of hope, a witness to the resurrection. How I wish our daughter rested in the peace of the place.

The cemetery slopes in several places, which can make the walk difficult in wet weather. It has been a dry couple of weeks, however, and I was able to follow Dylan as she raced down the incline from the children's to the married men's choir section. She had chased a field mouse in vain. Winded, we collected ourselves before the gravestones of William Meek Cummings and William Bryant Harris. The latter went by Bill.

Each man farmed independently, although I am sure there were a number of occasions in which one helped the other. It used to take an entire town to raise a barn. But by the time I arrived, William and Bill were barely speaking to each other.

It seems their dispute arose over a fence. According to Bill, he had repaired the wire for years while his neighbor had not bothered to lift so much as a finger. Or, was it the other way around? I have actually forgotten. I clearly remember how each man dug in his heels. William had always sat behind Bill in church. One morning,

I looked out on the congregation and saw him scowling in the opposite corner of the sanctuary. I did not grasp the full significance of this until later.

To a newcomer like me, the whole thing seemed ridiculous. How could a relationship deteriorate beyond repair over a little bit of fence? Fresh out of seminary, I thought I could remedy the situation. I never validated one side over the other. I thought I straddled the fence. But William began worshipping with the Lutherans in the next town. Nothing against those brothers and sisters, but this was a great sadness for our congregation, a loss which could not be grieved openly. Bill would hear none of it.

I remember both William and Bill with far more compassion now. Each man felt his integrity was on the line. They were proud men, sure of themselves, sure of their place in the world. There are times when I, too, long for such clarity.

But each man bore his pride down to the grave. One died within a week of the other, so they are buried side-by-side. Peaceful neighbors at the last, the modest tombstones bear silent witness in the same morning light.

The sixteenth of August has once again come and gone. I need to focus on my work for tomorrow's funeral, as well as for Sunday. But I am journaling because Dad called this morning. He wanted to wish me a happy anniversary. It is just like him to forget dates, so I reminded him of Philip's birthday tomorrow.

Dad continues to love Florida, bonefishing, margaritas. And the plethora of eligible women his age. I have observed my father in his habitat—a denizen of the land of retirement, he is tubby and orange and roots around beach bars, salivating over widows in unflattering sun dresses.

During his monthly phone call, I refrain from such judgments. We both tone down our language. We ask basic questions about health and well-being. And Dad can be charming. He has developed a genuine fondness for Bonnie. He dearly loves his grandsons. But Dad is as self-absorbed as a teenager, essentially too wrapped up in his own life to make much room for others. This selfishness is the nature of young men; it is disappointing in my father.

He shows absolutely no interest in church, which is at least consistent with my childhood. So I just tell him things at work are fine and inquire about his latest fishing excursion. And there is always baseball. I find that I step outside myself during these conversations, as if I am a scientist conducting field research about a peculiar evolution between generations.

Probably the best thing that happened to my relationship with my father is that I became one myself. Confronted with the challenges of my own children, I gained a new empathy for Dad.

Philip was colicky, which is another word for hell. One night, he woke up screaming like a banshee. Bonnie was assisting her recently widowed mother. I was on my own. For the next several hours, I paced and soothed, cooed and sung, prayed and cursed. Everything short of standing on my head. Nothing worked. Philip's face was turning purple. His gums were bared. I was completely repulsed. I saw myself throwing this monstrosity against the wall, pictured him sailing through the air, bouncing off the wallpaper, hitting the floor, and falling silent. This vision washed over me with such clarity that I literally started shaking from fear and had to set

Philip down in his crib. I then sank to my knees. No longer was I the prosecutor, skewering my father on the witness stand. I, too, was guilty.

As I have prayed for clemency, I have learned to pardon my father. I realize his abhorrence of the church is a safer outlet than loathing God. He is too proud to cry for help. I know Dad lost the love of his life, a gaping void that he can never fill, so he decorates the area around the dark pit with pleasures and niceties. I recognize he is coping and that it could be worse. We are alive and talking.

At promptly nine o'clock this morning, I spoke with Brother Marty by telephone, although we were no more than five feet from each other. My friend only wanted to talk about his garden, how he could not wait to get his hands in the dirt again. Predictably, he did not want to talk about his drinking and driving, which had landed him in prison several months ago.

Marty is the type of man we describe around here as a little rough around the edges, not only because he used to spit tobacco juice on the grass after Sunday's service. He obviously has substance abuse issues, yet he is dependable in most ways. I think of him as a large rock in the middle of a lake—solid and strong and possibly even alluring. But there is no place to dock safely. He has been divorced twice and has three daughters from three different women. That is enough, he says, to drive him to drink.

At Marty's insistence, I close our weekly time together with a reading from Paul's letter to the Corinthians, the famous love chapter. The same verses were read at my wedding and countless others I have officiated over the years. Marty was married in a Vegas chapel and a courthouse in Jackson, Mississippi. He has never held to convention. But while certainly a beautiful text, it struck me as a strange choice for the visitation cell. Yet the sound of the ancient words, echoing off the bare concrete walls, never fails to bring new beauty to them. Marty is not the most handsome man. His gap-toothed grin and squinty eyes are set off by elephant ears. During the reading, however, his face reminds me of a flower opened to the sun.

Due to these visitations, I have been absent from the Thursday morning Bible class. This group began at the prompting of Jimmy and Maggie Pulliam. Actually, all because of Sister Maggie. The boxes in my office were not even fully unpacked when she barged in, talking a mile a minute about how she had always wanted to read the Bible all the way through, from cover to cover, Genesis to Revelation, but as many times as she had started, she could never quite make it, either getting bogged down in the law code of Leviticus or the lists of kings in 2 Chronicles or something like that. Did I know what she was talking about? Of course, she was aware that the Daily Texts chart a course through the Bible in two years. But why not convene a weekly class that would read and discuss the scriptures, adding insight and holding one another accountable all the way through to the end?

"Don't the Bible say somewhere that there's strength in numbers, Reverend Wheeler? Well, all the more reason to have a class to read the Bible and find out where it says that exactly, right?"

In addition to her new pastor, Maggie Pulliam fast-talked two of the most faithful members of the church, Reverend Jennings and his wife, Irma. Jennings and I go way back—he was my pastor when I was a teenager. Back then, his greatest source of pride was that he almost never missed any church, any day of the week.

"If the doors are open, then I'm walking through," he would boast.

In retirement, the pull of grandchildren in Florida was strong. Perhaps it was his wife's turn to make the calendar and Bible study was not at the top of the list.

More people came and went as well. Some weeks, the class would swell to double digits; then, there would only be Jimmy, Maggie, and me. When the group first started, I would prepare ahead of class, bringing such things to study as Walter Brueggemann's reimagining of Israel's prophets and John Shelby Spong's work on the Jewishness of Jesus and Phyllis Trible's feminist biblical critique. I thought such thinkers were cutting edge and presented their ideas to prove myself to my former preacher and teacher. It took me awhile to figure out that no one was there to listen to me.

It took almost three years to read through the Bible. I will never forget that morning when we finished the Book of Revelation, reading the final benediction out loud together. There was a brief and heavy silence in the old Sunday school classroom. The clock chimed the hour. It was Brother Jimmy who finally spoke.

"Well, Reverend Wheeler, we'll see you next week. Genesis, chapter one."

They have not stopped reading.

This week they continue the Psalms, which marks the sixth time for Jimmy, the second since his beloved Maggie died. Shortly after her passing, we read the lament of Psalm 6:6. *All night long I flood my bed with weeping and drench my couch with tears.* Brother Jimmy broke down and we all cried for his loss. Later we read from Psalm 30. *Weeping may stay for the night, but rejoicing comes in the morning.* By this point, I had learned to let the Bible speak.

When I first met him, Jimmy Pulliam only came to church on the high holies—Easter, Christmas, Mother's Day. He is now a legend around here, the Talmage equivalent of the desert fathers of antiquity famed for their piety. I once met a Methodist bishop who, upon learning the church I served, wanted to know if it was true that a gentleman had memorized most of the Bible.

At Sister Maggie's original insistence, the group has always read from the New International Version. So it is not as though Jimmy—legend that he is—walks around dropping "thou" and "ye" into everyday conversations. He rarely quotes chapter and verse without prompting. But if one has the ears to hear, it is obvious how scripture peppers his language, flavors his words. Or, maybe the metaphor is that the Bible is like salt in the water of his speech—inseparable union.

Recently, I asked him to cite his favorite verse. He answered immediately, recalling from memory. *Love is patient; love is kind; love is not envious or boastful or arrogant. It is not rude, it is not self-seeking, it is not easily angered, it keeps no record of wrongs. Love does not delight in evil but rejoices with the truth.*

There are not many similarities between Jimmy and Marty. But they find comfort and inspiration in the same words. This speaks for itself.

———•———

Not long after returning from the jail, I looked up from my Bible to see a rotund, middle-aged, white woman with watery eyes filling the doorway to my office, a woman I had never seen before. Uninvited, she sat down in one of my wingback chairs and immediately began unburdening herself of her tale of woe about her former employment at a packing house where she had slipped a disk and could subsequently no longer work; and though this freak accident was no fault of hers, she did not receive her fair share of worker's compensation nor did those greedy sonofabitches in corporate headquarters cover her medical expenses; and so she had extra bills and no income and her fleabag husband had already hightailed it out of town with a trashy teenager from Philadelphia and God knows where he is now but she sure as hell knows he don't pay a dime of child support; and she has two boys to feed who are in elementary school and they eat her out of house and home and then, and so, and, and, and . . .

As I sat there, unable to insert so much as one word in edgewise, the better part of me attempted to channel what I have always imagined to be the Lord's look—a bright gaze of absolute love and compassion. Yeah, right. I confess my own eyes surely betrayed my frustration. She finally got down to the bottom of it. She needed financial assistance to keep her electricity on. She looked at me expectantly.

With a deep breath, I explained our church's policy, careful to avoid any implication that we were unsympathetic toward her plight, yet clear to stipulate that, as per stated policy, we exclusively gave money directly to social services. She then looked at me blankly. Assuming she did not understand, I re-launched my careful and clear speech. Again there was a vacuous look. Opening my desk drawer, I took out the business card of the woman in social services and offered to call, suggesting that she might be of more help. Brightening up, the woman asked if I might drive her to that office.

Good Lord. I had this afternoon to write Sunday's sermon. After Brother Ralph's service tomorrow, my boys are arriving. One afternoon is a wholly inadequate margin of time in which to address the holy obligation of Sunday morning. Yet this intruder was going to take even that from me. While attempting to compose myself in order to offer a legitimate excuse in my best pastoral tone of voice, I allowed a little flutter of silence in the space between us, which she filled.

"I don't mean to bother you, Pastor."

Damn.

When I first came to serve this parish, I heard a rumor about a member named Livingston who had recently sold all of his cattle and farming equipment. Reverend Jennings, the old pro, advised me that he did this in order to ensure that, unlike many farmers, he would stay retired. Unencumbered and unrestrained, Livingston passed his time by reading voraciously, engaging his active mind with a wide range of topics, most of which had very little to do with Christianity, much less the business of being a parish pastor, yet all of which he most earnestly sought to discuss with yours truly. He never called ahead to make an appointment. Livingston would stride into my office with a big smile.

"I don't mean to bother you, Wheeler. But you're in the business of being bothered, aren't you?"

Livingston has been dead now for a little more than two years. As I drove today's unannounced visitor to the downtown office of social services, I tried in vain to remember the exact date of his funeral. We buried him on an unusually warm day in early spring, which I recalled as I sat in yet another office and heard her very sad and very, *very* long story for the second time. As she went on and on, I recalled how I stood before Livingston's open grave, thinking how strange it was that I was shivering because it was not the least bit cold. It was only when my teeth began to chatter that I realized the extent of my grief. For here was my dear friend being lowered in the ground who would never again march into my office and interrupt my day to pontificate profusely about only God-knows-what and thereby pester me nearly to my wits end—all because he loved me and knew that I loved him.

Thanks to the competent and committed social worker, we managed to finagle a way to keep this woman's electricity on for the immediate future. Relief lit up her face. I said goodbye and God bless, as I paid her bus fare. The public transportation pulled away in a cloud of black smog. Fanning the exhaust from my line of vision, I glimpsed her face in the window. She was clearly grateful.

On returning to the church, I saw about a dozen little boys and girls gliding carefree all around the yard like bubbles in the breeze. I assumed their parents were busy setting up for the funeral inside. There is always much to be done. In fact, I was thinking of all that I had to do when one of the children ran up to me, excited and out of breath. I squatted down so that I could look him in the eye. I did not know this boy. He must have been part of the out of town family. When I reached out to shake his hand, he opened his fist to reveal an acorn resting in his little pink palm.

"Do you want to buy this from me?"

He had obviously scooped up the nut from the church grounds. I indicated that I might do the same. The little boy shook his head.

"No sir! That'd be bad for business."

Clearly, I was dealing with a real salesman. So I inquired about the price.

He spoke very solemnly. "Two dollars. I'm giving you such a good deal because Mommy says you're a preacher."

After confirming the truthfulness of his most reliable source, I inquired what I would do with said acorn, assuming that I did indeed purchase it from him at such a bargain price. His eyes widened and the words skipped out of him.

"That's the best part! You go home with it and dig it and plant it and dirt it and water it and then in *two days* it grows as big as . . . that!"

He pointed to an oak tree that had been growing on our church's property for at least a hundred years.

"That's why it's two whole dollars."

A few minutes later, I continued into the church with less money in my wallet. But I had been bothered toward something holy—two times in one afternoon. Can it be that child-like innocence is earned? Is that what Jesus meant by commanding us to have the faith of one of the little ones, the least among us?

I planted that acorn on my way home. I can see the exact spot through the window from where I write. I got my hands in the dirt, as Marty would have put it. I should be writing a sermon, but something about that boy has reminded me of my incarcerated friend.

Marty grew up in this church. Every Christmas, he would hike the mountains slathered so thick with evergreens that old-timers refer to the place as "Black Hollar" because it is under perpetual shade. Our worship space is roughly twenty feet tall, a dimension Marty knows full well. But he would still come back with a thirty-footer and cram it through the doors, employing a chainsaw to make necessary alterations. Always the same, year after year, even after two marriages, two divorces, and three children. Brother Marty was still a part of the Christmas magic. He is family.

When my sons reached elementary school, they were allowed to go up the mountain with Marty and his boisterous daughters, including the youngest, the beautiful Delilah. I was waiting when my boys burst into the sanctuary.

"Daddy, we got the biggest one!"

There was Marty close behind, the hint of a hint of a smile on his face.

"Yes, we did. And they picked it out."

Nathaniel and Philip stuck out their bird-like chests with pride. I have Marty to thank for that. So much of prayer is a calling to mind.

———•———

After supper, Bonnie and I took our Dylan for a walk, delighting in the unexpected coolness of one of the dog days of summer. As we approached the church, I saw about a dozen unknown vehicles parked in the gravel lot. On Sunday mornings, I invariably recognize every car. Thursdays are for anonymity.

The twelve-step program has met at Talmage Moravian for almost a decade now. Scanning the parking lot, I mused about how many cars must have graced our humble lot over the years. Bonnie took my hand and squeezed it.

Our governing board affirms the group's annual request for the use of our fellowship hall. Permission is granted unanimously. The church of the basement, we have come to call it. But initially, there was considerable debate among our elected lay leaders. While a few voiced cautious support, others expressed what I am sure they felt were valid concerns. What about the power bill? What about the custodian's duties? Why can't they use another church, maybe a bigger one? Who'll unlock the door and who'll lock it back? Someone raised a concern about the safety of the children—despite the fact that we did not host any programs on Thursday night and had no plans whatsoever to do so.

The discussion was already in its second hour when Livingston, uncharacteristically silent, spoke for the first time. As he called for attention, all eyes shifted toward him in the back of the room. He leveled his gaze directly at me.

"What about you, Wheeler? Do you think this is a good idea?"

I nodded firmly, prepared to offer my rationale for hosting the least of those among us. Brother Livingston held up his hand for silence.

"That's all I need. I still have questions, but I trust you more."

Enough time in one place and you earn something more than a salary.

At the beginning, however, the congregation made me work harder. For months, I alone was responsible for unlocking the door to the fellowship hall and returning two hours later to close up again. I did these duties, albeit with growing resentment. This was before Marty's troubles were fully known, so while I believed in the group in principle, I did not think I had a personal stake in our congregation's involvement. And I certainly had other responsibilities. If it had been left solely to me, I suspect the church of the basement would be meeting somewhere else this evening.

But Marjorie Stemlich came by the house just as I was about to head over. She told me not to bother because she was going to the church anyway. I thanked her and innocently asked why she happened to be here this evening. Blushing bright red, she mumbled something about needing to practice the hymns for Sunday. I started to say something about how choir practice was only yesterday and, besides, she had never practiced before. But I merely smiled. I figured I would find out eventually.

Marjorie's old Chevy is the only car I recognize in the parking lot, though I know she has been taking Delilah to the meetings. Not even Marjorie, though, has been able to convince Delilah's father, Marty. Perhaps this will change upon his release.

"You know, Wheeler, we can be repaired," said Marjorie last Thursday when we crossed paths on her way to meeting. "It's like how a damaged book receives a new spine."

She smiled because I knew she was quoting Bonnie.

At her invitation, I was there when Marjorie received her green sobriety chip for her first ninety days and then again at the awarding of the bronze chip for her first year. I have heard her speak many times, which I consider to be one of the great privileges anyone in the church has ever bestowed upon me. It is humbling to think about all the telltale signs I overlooked: the pile of empty aspirin bottles inside the piano bench, the stumbling into produce displays in the grocery store, the evasive responses to casual questions. I chalked up all these things and more to, well, that's just Marjorie being Marjorie. We all did that, friends and family alike, her brothers and sisters in Christ. Our minding our own business might have killed her.

Love is patient, love is kind. The church of the basement has taught me about telling the truth in love—truth like a newborn's purple-face, bared-gum, banshee scream. Truth confronts you. It may strip away your pride. It may even wound you. But an open wound may heal into a scar. And you can share a story about a scar.

Maybe I got to work on my sermon today after all.

Nathaniel and Philip have each promised to be home by supper time.

When the boys were young, I used to call back over my shoulder on my way out the door. *Don't worry, I'll be back later.* Deep down, I realized that promise was not mine to guarantee, but that is what I always said.

Like father, like son. Every time they leave for college, they blithely promise to return. "Don't worry," they add, as if speaking such words would make them true. Don't worry? How could they ask that? Blissfully reckless in youth's illusion of immortality, the prospect of return is never in question.

But deep, deep down they know the truth.

As young boys, Nathaniel and Philip would play this game with their mother every single time they prepared to cross a street. Whether before a deserted gravel road or busy intersection, they would slam on their foot breaks at the very edge and yell at the top of their lungs, "Stop!" Their arms would flail out sideways like an umpire signaling safe. "Look left! Look right! Look left!" Their necks whipped back and forth and back again. This was entirely Bonnie's idea. The whole production seemed needlessly dramatic to me.

I had driven Nathaniel and Philip to the video rental store with the promise they could select any movie their hearts desired—any G-rated movie, that is. My boys viewed those shelves lined with VHS cassettes as the heavenly banquet table, which was the topic that I was working on for the next morning's worship. So I handed over the cash and sent them inside alone in order to continue my sermon preparation in the car.

Not long after, I glanced up from my notes and saw them fling open the store's glass double doors. They were shrieking with excitement as they raced down the sidewalk toward the car. An instant later, I saw the delivery van fly around a corner.

I was plastered to the seat. Even the screams were trapped in my throat.

But the boys stopped at the very edge of the curb.

The van rushed by, the wind whipping their hair out of their eyes.

If either Nathaniel or Philip had registered any danger, it was completely forgotten by the time we pulled into our driveway and they bounded out of the car like puppies. I still shiver at the memory of that close call.

As for today, I have promised to be at the church in a few minutes for the funeral. Nathaniel and Philip have promised to drive carefully. I will try not to worry, as Bonnie has taught me.

—••—

The Skews family has been burying people in our community since the early part of the nineteenth century. They remember the influenza outbreak of 1918, an epidemic of biblical proportions when graves could not be dug fast enough. When he was a boy, Richard Skews was hired to sit up all night with the deceased who were laid out in wooden caskets inside people's homes, usually in the dining room. Skews, as we know him today, calls every man younger than him "Honey" and every young woman "Ma'am" and every boy "Billy" and every girl "Susie" and all widows by their full names. He also loves heavy metal music and punk rock. We stood outside the church before the service, motioning cars where to park.

"Honey, remember this name. The Mooney Suzuki. Just awesome, let me tell you."

It was typical funeral weather—gray and gloomy. As Skews continued to sing the praises of this band, I nodded absentmindedly, holding a large umbrella to shield both of us from the steady drizzle. I do not like the electric guitar, not even Dylan, but I humor my friend. I was genuinely amused by the thought that the funeral goers might have assumed the two of us were engaged in some weighty topic as they drove by in great solemnity.

"The guitarist shreds and the drummer, why, he tears it up! I dropped two hundred on them for November. Honey, if that don't tell you something, what will?"

Unless they have prior experience with a loved one's death, few are aware of how grief clouds the mind, rendering the simplest decisions nearly impossible. Clucking his tongue sympathetically, Skews has shared stories about shocked widowers entering his office in mismatched socks and half-buttoned shirts. With patience and dignity, he guides mourners through those shell-shocked days immediately after death. Honey, I tell people, Skews is the best.

But Lord knows he cannot talk about funerals all day long, even if death is his living.

We shifted to his other favorite topic, the Pittsburgh Pirates. He and I are unlikely allies in this region of Philadelphia Phillies devotees. Skews wondered if Ralph Jibsen had been a baseball man.

"Maybe cause a few to bounce our way from his new box seats?"

Baseball is timeless. There are no periods or quarters or even clocks, which makes the sport ideally suited for eternity. But I regret to note that the deceased had been a diehard Phillies fan and had sworn to remain faithful throughout all the ages.

"Honey, many a good man's been wasted on those Phillies," Skews groaned.

As for the here and now, we passed the duration of the morning demonizing Barry Bonds, once our hero, now traitor for the San Francisco Giants. I know a man of better faith would wish our former player well. It is hard to rise to Christ's level of forgiveness when your team is at the bottom of the standings.

I first met Skews at a funeral, of course. The service for Betsy's baby. Only family and the closest of friends had been invited. I remember reading Psalm 40 and hearing the echo of my usually high-pitched voice, which sounded rhythmic and low like a bass drum that day.

Comfort ye, comfort ye my people, saith your God.

As we prepared to recess from the front of sanctuary, I noticed the funeral director happened to stand beside Betsy. She was wearing a simple black dress. Her mascara was smeared all across her face. I watched, transfixed, as that man leaned in and whispered. Her bloodshot eyes widened and she actually smiled, her stained cheeks turning upward in a little miracle of tragic wonder. She took his arm and Skews escorted her down the aisle. I made a special trip to the funeral home a few days later, specifically to ask what in the world he had said. Skews shook his head.

"Honey, I don't even remember."

We have been close ever since.

Meeting with the Jibsen family before the funeral today, I offered my condolences and pledged my assistance in any way possible. I say these things every single time and all eyes glaze over. But mourners respond to a hand on the shoulder, tearfully whisper their gratitude for a breath mint or a tissue. I recently told Skews

I thought of our work as providing handrails for those who are grieving.

"Honey, you sure talk more than any old handrail!"

Of course, there are plenty of words offered, prayed, and sung over the course of a funeral service. But the Moravian liturgy is not as long as some of the higher church traditions, such as the Episcopalian or Roman Catholic. Maybe writing this down will remind me to point that out to Skews.

While I appreciate a modicum of spontaneity in worship, particularly if it is heartfelt, there is good precedent for offering the same prayers over and over: when you pray, Jesus taught, pray like this. The Lord's Prayer does not change and I would sooner trust what has stood the test of time, what has born the weight of human experience. The repetition also suggests that we approach the same words in different ways, depending on the situation and condition of our hearts. The uniform structure allows freedom for each of us to be true to ourselves and yet find wholeness in something larger—e pluribus unum.

I have led the Moravian liturgy countless times. The congregation dutifully responds in unison. Perhaps there are parts which seem rote or impersonal. But it never fails that a couple of the familiar words will stand out, as if underlined in bright red. During Brother Ralph's service, this was true of the phrase serve Christ in eternal righteousness, innocence, and happiness.

Righteousness is a word that one would expect. It is hard to read even a few pages of Paul's letters without encountering the term. A churchy word, too. The kind of thing we say all the time about God and ourselves even if we do not know what it means. That is the danger of a familiar liturgy—a dulling of the intellect, a rehearsing of the mystery unfathomable.

But innocence and happiness! What were those words doing there? What do such terms mean in the context of a funeral liturgy, the heavy lifting of hope by faithful people in the broken and bruised world?

As I read Brother Ralph's lebenslauf, I was aware of people listening who knew these details by heart. Many, especially his beloved, had treasured the man in their hearts. And yet, this was his spiritual autobiography, not merely a summary of the course of his life, but his faith writ large.

Brother Ralph had left specific instructions that a sealed envelope should only be opened and read during his funeral. When I explained this, nervous electricity shot through the congregation. Sister Helen allowed me to make a copy after the service was over. Such words of courageous vulnerability should be preserved.

My dearest Helen, do you remember when we was first married and we'd try to wake up first? Before the other? You'd want to fix me a big breakfast before work, but sometimes I'd get up quietly and beat you to the kitchen. I can't even fry an egg, you know. I waited in the kitchen to see your smile when you come through the door. I just loved waiting for you.

I paused at this point and stole a glance at her. She was barely breathing. And she wore her grief and gratitude in a way that—far, far in the future—I hope will be true of Bonnie.

Now, Helen, you and me has been through a lot over the years. I'm sorry I won't be here anymore with you. But I hope you live a long, long life and that your days are full and bright.

And dear, I'd like for you to think of my death as getting up before you. When it's time, I'll be waiting.

The congregation responded in unison with an unscripted sigh. Notes of innocence and happiness from beyond the grave.

"Honey, I have never in all my life," Skews commented to me at the reception.

When the boys were both in high school, they had to be home before midnight. Philip begged, bargained, and occasionally raged for a later hour. But we held firm. In light of Sunday morning, I should have been in bed long before then, but I could never relax until I heard the key in the door and footsteps padding softly down the hall. Since sleep was futile, I developed a habit of working on my sermon during those late hours of waiting. My anxiety bled onto those pages.

I have been attempting to work on my sermon this afternoon while waiting once again for their return. From the same window in my office where I used to stare into the dark, willing my boys safely home, I now look into this suddenly sun-soaked afternoon. Philip's powder blue Subaru has pulled into our driveway with Nathaniel's red pick-up following immediately behind. They have greeted each other with a hearty hug, laughing loudly enough for me to hear.

What's a homecoming without a feast?

Worship was the bread and butter of the early Moravian community. The brothers and sisters at Herrnhut spent so much time together in prayer that the need arose to eat; and so the Lovefeast was born, an extension of corporate worship, an echo of meals shared among the believers in the New Testament. For our family, Bonnie prepared homemade pizza, using fresh tomatoes from her garden for the sauce. August is a red, ripe month. And she baked the crust from scratch. Pulling the pizza piping hot from the oven, Bonnie sprinkled some of her homegrown basil and oregano on top before adding a little feta cheese. A passerby outside our kitchen window would propose to Bonnie based on aroma alone.

After this feast of love, Bonnie insisted on clearing the table, whisking the empty plates into the kitchen in order to grace me with the blessed company of our two sons. I cracked open a beer for each of us and we moved into the living room. We toasted Philip and settled into chairs around the coffee table to lament the ineptitude of our Pirates and curse Barry Bonds.

But Nathaniel felt the need to shift topic, stating he no longer believes it is essential to one's salvation to attend church. My son swigged his beer. He had that look in his eyes. Here we go.

"Organized religion," Nathaniel stated with a professorial air, "has been the downfall of Christianity, manipulating and corrupting the teachings of Jesus for human gain and power. Besides, the rituals are ancient, the language outdated. Liturgies are so boring, merely saying the same thing over and over."

I winced but Nathaniel was picking up steam.

"If the church stands a prayer of connecting with a new generation, then people need new music, new prayers, new ways of living their faith!"

Nathaniel's refrain reminded me of a chick in the nest, chirping away—new, new, new. My son is now ingesting theological nourishment different than what he had been raised on. But I did recognize the truth and merit of his revelations because, ironically, they are nothing new. I heard such arguments when I was in college.

I struggle with the line between tradition and innovation, familiar and fresh, when planning every service.

But before I had the chance even to slip in a word edgewise, the birthday boy emphatically responded to his brother's impromptu homily. Reaching for another beer, Philip declared that his brother was not taking his conclusions far enough!

"Yes, the church is outdated and hopelessly so. But religion itself is the product of a pre-Enlightenment age, the mythical thinking of our ancestors, those primitive cultures without access to the scientific method. If one is not equipped with legitimate means of ascertaining the truth, then fabricated stories are attractive alternatives."

Attractive alternatives?

"That's right, Dad. You fake it until you make it," Philip spat with a biting laugh. "Religious indoctrination, then, has been a hallmark of human societies. But we as a human civilization can no longer afford that option."

"What are you saying?" Nathaniel demanded.

"Religion has outlived its purpose," Philip retorted, voice rising as if in the pulpit. "Such superstitions only lead to violence, as people kill one another over competing truth claims. How tragic when the deeper truth is that all religions are based entirely upon fiction!"

Entirely upon fiction?

"Absolute fiction, Dad! That's the truth!"

Over their shoulders, I saw Bonnie peak into the room. The boys were staring at me. Perhaps they recalled other times when I have taken the emotional bait—hook, line, and sinker. Upon reflection, I wonder how much of this conversation was merely intended for provocation. *What will you do with this, Dad? Your move, old man!* I well remember the exhilaration of self-righteous indignation against your father, working him into a lather of sputtering protest. It is strangely satisfying, but also fool's gold, shiny and petty. Mean hopes and cheap pleasures are merely that. And I no longer believe I am nearly as smart as I used to think I was—a complicated sentence and a blessing limping forward.

Bonnie was still hidden from their view. I told Nathaniel and Philip how I appreciated the fact that my sons were being taught to think for themselves. Part of self-discovery is questioning what you have been told. Did they perhaps remember the story of their biblical namesakes? Nathaniel asked his brother, Philip, if anything good could come from Nazareth. And what was the response?

"Come and see," they recited in unison like bored students. I caught Bonnie smiling at me. *Go on.* Her green eyes sparkled. *I'm rooting for you.*

I recalled for Nathaniel and Philip the summers when Steve and Marty erected a mailbox in the backyard of the parsonage so that people in the congregation could deliver treasures. Like turkey feathers and shark teeth, remember? At their request that repository was spray-painted orange one year and God-awful-neon purple the next. Did they remember opening its creaky door, revealing Christmas in July?

They did not seem to be listening, but I pressed on.

When their mother went back to graduate school and night classes, a different person from the church would bring food every Tuesday night. And not just any food! Their favorites—fried chicken and biscuits, made from scratch mashed potatoes and gravy, homemade spaghetti sauce, macaroni and cheese—Lord knows, not from the box! Now my boys were smiling, albeit faintly. Did they remember Patsy Miller's double-fudge brownies? How we could never ever eat just one? Chuckles of appreciation.

Bonnie bounced into the room.

"I hear laughter. Are we ready to tell our joke?"

Nathaniel and Philip groaned. "Not the Moravian dog!"

"Come on! Indulge your mother after she has fed you supper."

They would have told the joke anyway. I forget where I heard it, but it is one of our oldest running family traditions. Nathaniel always starts.

"There was once a Moravian pastor who received a phone call from a little old lady requesting his assistance that afternoon regarding a matter of utmost urgency."

I interjected here, clarifying that the pastor dutifully obliged her request, although this woman was not a member of his church. This detail is important. Philip picked up the narrative from there.

"Tearfully, this dear lady explained that her beloved dog of the past fifteen years had died that very morning. 'Oh my goodness, dear gracious honorable Reverend! Would you be ever so kind as to hold, pretty please, the tiniest little funeral for this dearly departed dog of mine?'"

Lays it on thick! He has a flair for the dramatic. Cue Nathaniel.

"This pastor politely declined, offering his heartfelt condolences."

"But wouldn't you know it?" Philip continued. "The woman was insistent! Seeking to extricate himself from this bothersome situation, the Moravian pastor volunteered the name and phone number of a Presbyterian minister in the same town."

This always makes me laugh. I have been telling this joke since seminary, but the pastor used to be Methodist. That one detail changed after I met McPherson.

"So the old lady thanked him," Nathaniel added. "But she wondered if she might ask one more question."

Philip again. "'Oh gracious honorable Reverend! In your educated and esteemed opinion, do you believe that five hundred dollars is adequate compensation for a pet's funeral?'"

Then everyone in the family cries out the punch line, quoting the pastor.

"'Wait a minute! You didn't tell me that you had a *Moravian* dog!'"

The ritual complete, Bonnie requested help in the kitchen. Nathaniel and Philip were smiling as they left the room.

Bonnie gave me a kiss. Not a perfunctory smooch, but a kiss with some staying power.

When the kitchen was clean, the boys lured me into the backyard with baseball and gloves. I intended a game of catch as part of our friendly homecoming. But Nathaniel insisted on playing the game of their childhood—Burnout. Bonnie refers to this long running tradition as a full-out display of testosterone. The simple premise is to throw the ball back and forth as hard as you can, and then remove the baseball gloves to determine whose hand is the reddest. Ever since they hit puberty, I have always been declared the winner.

Mercifully, Bonnie entered once again. She came and poured red wine, which helps soothe the pain from a red palm.

"Remember what the rabbis say, boys. 'There's no joy without wine.'"

She loves that quote.

She also brought homemade chocolate cake with caramel icing, the birthday boy's favorite. We enjoyed the food and drink underneath the cathedral of majestic oaks. The cicadas are amazing this time of year. The seemingly random and inchoate sound of one arouses the entire orchestra to perform at full strength. Grace sneaks up on you like that. Like how the stars appear.

Bonnie handed Philip his birthday card. Her legs bounced excitedly as Philip, ever the card himself, opened the envelope excruciatingly slow. Finally, Bonnie had enough.

"Come on already!"

Philip tore open the envelope with a flourish and held the card for all to see. On the cover was a picture of a chicken. The inside read: *You are twenty-one! That's so clucking awesome!* He knew exactly who was responsible that brand of witticism.

"Thanks Mom, I love it!"

But Philip thanked both of us when he noticed the check that had fluttered to the ground. He has always been genuinely grateful. For his fifth birthday, Grandmother Lois gave him a gift concealed in a bag with tissue paper. Little Philip squealed with delight.

"You gave me tissues to blow my nose!"

I think of little Timothy and Bud Thompson. A child's innocence is the greatest gift, a reminder of what we once had and, possibly, what we might yet be.

Nathaniel is calling me back outside. Enough for tonight. My heart, head, and stomach are full.

I had not intended to return to my writing before bed. But what has happened was not at all expected. Lord, it is painful to remember for so many reasons. I have been unable to pray. I do not know what to say to God.

I am striving for peace in ink. And tears.

I fully intended to say good night. Nathaniel stood up and cleared his throat. Philip had been teasing me about having too much to drink, but the look on my other son's face wiped away all smiles. My insides knotted. I could tell this was serious. Had he relapsed? Was he in trouble at school?

"I am a Christian, and I am gay."

Before I had picked my jaw off the ground, Bonnie jumped to her feet and wrapped her arms around Nathaniel's neck. She squeezed him for all she was worth!

"My dear, I love you! I love you always!"

Now that I think about it, she might have meant *I love you, all ways.*

"Thanks Mom," Nathaniel managed, his voice cracking.

Several beats passed before I realized that Bonnie was glaring at me. *Get off your butt.* I walked briskly over to Nathaniel and, well, kind of stood there. I could not meet his eyes. Staring at the ground, I remembering thinking that I should hug him, yes, that is the right thing for a father to do. But my arms seemed too heavy to lift. I do not remember what I said.

I moved aside quickly. Philip stepped up and embraced his brother. Pulling back, he put his hands on Nathaniel's shoulders. They are almost the exact same height. Perfect for locking eyes.

"Dude, you're gay? Are you, well, sure about this?"

I swear that even the cicadas fell silent.

"As sure as anything my whole life."

Writing helps. My heart has stopped racing, so there is a start.

If I am honest, this is no surprise. But if I am even more honest, I was hoping against hope that my intuition was wrong.

Bonnie and I are liberal. Not just the Bill Clinton, don't ask, don't tell kind either. Her graduate advisor, George, was Bonnie's mentor and confidant. He guided her through school and helped secure her job after graduation. George breaks all the stereotypes about dull librarians. He is vivacious, the life of every party. We have shared some great times with him and his beloved.

God, I am trying to justify myself. It seems like everyone has a gay friend. But still . . .

On the first evening we were invited to their home, George met us at the door in a handsome blue suit. He wore a white flower in his lapel. He bowed and gestured grandly for us to enter. Purple orchids grew from stoneware in the middle of the foyer. The opposite wall was adorned with a beautiful watercolor of an Italian vineyard. Another gentleman promptly came down the marble staircase. Black suit. Pink flower. I remember the way George dramatically cleared his throat.

"Reverend Wheeler, may I present my love, Allen."

I told them to call me, Jaime, and gave Allen a hug. At future parties, whenever someone would raise an eyebrow at the mention of my profession, George would tell that story.

"Jaime is a dear. He's not like most of them."

Why did I not embrace my son?

I know something about prejudice and bigotry. Not personally, of course. But I know enough to realize that people are cruel, callous, uncaring. So often these people are men and women of faith. That is the painful truth behind George's comment. O Christ, save Nathaniel from those who would hurt him in your name!

I know the wage-of-sin-is-death lines of biblical interpretations. McPherson and I have discussed what he refers to as "clobber texts" because the Presbyterians are constantly beating one another over the head, wrangling over the issue of homosexuality from every conceivable point of view. That must be exhausting. McPherson is an articulate ally on behalf of the gay community. He once told me that bigotry can be a form of misdirected righteousness. Always cerebral, he explains the historical circumstances of the ancient world, including what certain words mean in the original language.

I know enough to understand that the Bible is not condemning loving, healthy relationships between any two people. Neither should I. This seems obvious. I am guided by the motto of our

Moravian Church: *in essentials, unity; in non-essentials, liberty; in all things, love.* McPherson laughs and says I am so very Moravian. Scholarship can illuminate, I know, but it is the story that carries the light.

I think about Ralph and Helen. You hear a story about trying to wake up first and you know that is love—the selfless sacrifice that Jesus taught. Such a story lodges a lump in your throat and prickles goose bumps across your arms. George and Allen have that kind of effect on me. Their love is that obvious. I can see that clearly.

But very few people at church or in our community know about my friendship with George and Allen. These men do not live nearby and we rarely work or socialize in the same circles. And I almost never mention them.

What will my son say about me?

I am a Christian, and I am gay.

How brave he is.

How typical I am. Pointing to my gay friends. Talking about the issue in the abstract. George was mistaken—I am one of them.

He is my son.

How timid I must seem to him. How small and selfish and scared.

I fear for Nathaniel.

During one AA meeting, Marjorie shared that her dad had tried to "beat the gay out" of her when she wore overalls as an adolescent. In college, two upperclassmen took turns raping her in an upstairs room at a fraternity party. A half dozen people gathered to taunt and jeer. "Therapy," they had called it. They were screaming, "Convert the queer!"

"But this is who I am," she concluded that night in the church of the basement, bearing witness to the truth. It was almost more than I could hear.

I do believe Marjorie when she says such things. I believe in her. She is who God made her to be. But except for the church in the basement, Marjorie remains closeted about her sexuality. She is not hiding anything per se, as she is not in a relationship. And most people at Talmage Moravian are likely aware. We just do not talk about such things. The pastor never brings it up. What would people say?

I think I am afraid of the answer. I suppose that fear pinned my arms to my sides tonight instead of embracing Nathaniel.

What does my son think about me?

I cannot sleep.

I think of another time when I did touch my son. At Nathaniel's confirmation, I placed my hand on his forehead and uttered his watchword, Jeremiah 29:11. *For I know the plans that I have for you, declares the Lord, plans to prosper you, not to harm you, plans to give you hope and a future.*

I had saved that verse for my firstborn even before Bonnie became pregnant again. I thought it was perfect. I believe those words have shone for Nathaniel while journeying down some dark roads. But as I read them once again just now, it is clear that the "I" in this verse is not me.

I am a Christian, and I am gay.

Some of Philip's high school buddies picked him up. They headed to one of the local bars. These young men always seem up to trouble. But what was I was going to say? He is clucking twenty-one, after all.

After his brother left, I sat with Nathaniel on our living room sofa. Only a couple of hours ago, we had told jokes from the very same seats. Bonnie kissed the top of his head and left to get ready for bed. It was late. Nathaniel looked at me, expectantly. I had not failed completely out there in the backyard. So much can hinge on only a few precious words between fathers and sons. This was such a time.

But I had no idea what to say.

Perhaps something theological would have been appropriate. I could have recited a fitting scripture from memory. Why did his watchword not occur to me then?

Without a doubt, I absolutely should have said, Nathaniel, I love you always and in all ways. We could have figured the rest out from there, working it out with fear and trembling perhaps.

Maybe I should have kept my mouth shut and been attentive. If only I had reached out and embraced him like his mother.

But I ended up retelling the story of how his mother had proposed to me in the bleachers. *You, James Wheeler, will marry me!*

I laughed. Nathaniel did not.

What did I expect? I am not sure what I was thinking. Probably, I was over-thinking. That particular memory has been on my mind, I guess. That was another time when I was scared. Like Nathaniel, Bonnie had been brave in telling her truth and that made all the difference. So I wanted to share something of that, something of my story in the effort to relate to Nathaniel's.

Nathaniel was still and quiet. We were seated so close that our legs were touching. I lifted my left arm over his shoulders and squeezed him. But suddenly his right hand pushed against my chest!

"You really don't get it, do you?"

As I fell against the couch cushion, Nathaniel shot to his feet. He mumbled something about going out to meet Philip. I stood and asked him to wait. Please. I tried to stop him by grabbing his elbow. But he twisted violently and wrenched out of my grasp. I lost my balance and stumbled. Pain shot through my ankle as I somehow managed to remain upright.

"Leave me alone, Dad!"

I let him go without another word.

For I know the plans that I have for you, declares the Lord, plans to prosper you, not to harm you, plans to give you hope and a future.

Now I am alone, nursing my wounds.

This dream.

Hear an engine roaring. Tires screeching. See a red truck. Know it is Nathaniel. Feel myself yelling for him to stop. My scream is silent. He zooms off.

I burst through my office window, shattering the glass, and hit the ground running. Never run so fast before. Can't believe how fast I am going. But the truck keeps receding further and further away until, suddenly, I launch myself into the air, rising above the road, soaring over the treetops.

See from a bird's eye view. A red dot below, his vehicle, begins side-winding. No time to scream. Nosedive. Wind rushing all around. Grab hold of the rear bumper with both hands. Pull. Pull hard. Pull with everything I have. But the truck overcorrects and loses control, skidding sharply off a cliff.

Free fall. Screaming, tumbling, somersaulting, a sickening whirl of sky and rock and tree and truck and me. A blur of colors and fear.

Stop. We have landed.

I come to myself lying on a blanket of soft snow. Up ahead, the truck comes to life, its taillights clicking on. As it drives slowly forward, a gentle powder is dislodged from the rear tires. I realize I had let go of the fender. And I woke up.

I recorded this dream after journeying slowly to my desk on my hurting ankle. I wrote by the light of the moon streaming through the window. I wanted to get everything down on paper. I climbed back into bed gingerly, trying not to wake Bonnie. But she rolled over with a grunt. The angry bed roll. Sleep was futile.

Studying my summary in this morning light, there is a fairly obvious meaning, even to a novice interpreter. I want to protect Nathaniel, but I realize I need to let go even as I cling tighter. This seems to be my problem at every stage of his life. No need to page Dr. Freud. Except for this nagging feeling about the unlikely appearance of snow in my midsummer night's dream.

She knew snow cream was my favorite treat. But Mom used to say that I should never eat the first snow—some old superstition, I guess. I pleaded with her, but to no avail. When the second storm finally hit, she would race around our backyard, her arms extended like the wings of an airplane. Her giggle rang like a bell in the cold air. As I chased behind, she would call over her shoulder. I can still hear her voice.

"Catch me if you can! Go, Jaime, go!"

She would dance, waving her arms, her head thrown back, laughing loudly. Once our Tupperware containers were about halfway full, we would stir in sugar and milk right then and there on the lawn. Her recipe seemed so simple, but I have never been able to recapture the exact deliciousness of her snow cream with my boys. How I have tried.

Mom was the neighborhood champion on the sled, too. She would launch her Flexible Flyer downhill at breakneck speed.

"Catch me if you can! Go, Jaime, go!"

Her shout would fade as she flew ahead, beating me and the rest of the neighborhood kids to the bottom. By the time I came down, she would already be racing back up, pulling her sled behind her.

It is not her fault that she died. But she was always leaving me behind.

I have often wondered what advice Mom would have shared as I have tried to parent my children. Snow cream and sleds will only take you so far.

Some say that boys marry their mothers. Bonnie, however, does not like snow. Not one bit.

———•———

The boys staggered in for breakfast not too long ago. Their mother had made her specialty pancakes, but they were intent on coffee. Clearly, they had a few more last night. I drank less but was not faring much better. My ankle is swollen from my stumble as Nathaniel was leaving. I also felt drugged and sluggish.

This morning was one of the quietest we have ever shared as a family. Not one single laugh.

Nathaniel had eaten about two bites when he laid down his silverware with a clatter and announced he was leaving. He shrugged off our protests, claiming that he needed to get back for work. The rest of us waited wordlessly in the kitchen while he gathered up his things. The only sound was an occasional scraping fork as we pushed our food around our plates.

Nathaniel stood in the threshold of the front door. His Pirates duffel bag was slung over his slumped shoulders. The three of us lined up to say our goodbyes. Philip gave him a bear hug. Bonnie squeezed his neck and kissed his left cheek. As often as I have watched, she has preferred that particular side.

My turn. I shook his right hand. Wished him the best. And told him what I should have said last night.

I. Love. You. Son.

Nathaniel stared at a spot somewhere over my left shoulder, away from his mother and brother, avoiding all eye contact. I looked him full in the face. He looks the most like my own mother.

He spun on his right heel. I followed him down the front walkway, limping after him. I struggled for words, too. Did you collect all of your belongings? Do you want some food for the road? Well, drive safely. Call if you need anything. Let us know when you arrive? He threw up his right hand in acknowledgment. But Nathaniel never turned around. I watched until his truck climbed over the ridge at the end of the street and dropped out of sight.

Even the weather is grey and muggy. Oppressive, really. Dylan sat at Philip's feet, not mine. Man's best friend regarded me with a look of mild disgust. As for my better half, Bonnie soon excused herself, muttering about the dirty dishes. I suspect she was crying, but I do not know for sure. She has not spoken one word to me since Nathaniel left.

I hobbled behind Philip into the backyard. I sat down and propped up my foot on another lawn chair. He began tossing a Frisbee for Dylan. After a few throws, Philip said that he did not want to talk about Nathaniel.

"That's why you're out here, huh, Dad?"

Fair enough. So I asked my youngest son about his future. He declared a business major this past spring. He was pledging a fraternity this fall. Did he have anything else in mind? I promised myself I would keep it positive.

Dylan plopped down in the grass, her pink tongue hanging out. Philip now seemed game for conversation. He hoped to pick up a minor in economics, possibly a double major. This was impressive. But he brushed off the praise, informing me that he did not care what he did as long as he made a lot of money doing it!

Philip raised his eyebrows. *Your move, old man.*

Like my Moravian forbearers, I harbor deep suspicions regarding anything that whiffs of ostentatious materialism. It is a nervous tick that I displayed for his entire childhood and adolescence. The embrace of fatherhood—the halfway hug with the push.

"Well, how might I support you, Philip?"

I surprised even myself. For once, I blurted out what came to mind.

He was looking at me as though I had sprouted another head. So I added that, of course, I want you to be successful, son. Why, with the ever-diminishing pension plan in the Moravian Church, you will have to take care of your dear old dad in his dotage! That drew a smile.

Philip picked up the Frisbee from the ground and tossed it once more across the yard. Dylan was unmoved. He ruefully acknowledged that we might not want him to spend the birthday money on his fraternity dues. Thank you for that, son. But I reminded him of the motto of the Moravian Church. He nodded and looked away. He has heard that before.

"I do have some advice for you, Dad. About Nathaniel."

The birds sung a measure or two in the trees above.

"You know what? I mean, money's great and all. But what I'd really like is for you to be there for me. You know, just come when I call you. No questions asked."

I jerked upright in my chair. Name one time, I demanded defensively, when he had asked me to be there and I had failed to do so.

"I don't know. Christ, Dad. You're not getting what I'm saying. What do you think Nathaniel wants from you anyway?"

From the time when he first began to talk, Philip has shrugged his right shoulder before speaking. Bonnie claims the gesture helps him think.

"Look, it's not rocket science. I mean, what did Jesus say? If someone is thirsty, give him a cup of cold water. If hungry, a hunk of bread. Right? Least thy brethren and all that. In plain English, that just means be there. Show up for your people. Am I right?"

That hit me in the chest, as Oak Arnold would say.

My youngest son has returned to school. Bonnie left without a word. I do not know where she went or when she will return. I am ready to limp to the church. I still have to be ready for Sunday's service.

———•———

I have not worked on my sermon.

Instead, I was remembering Nathaniel at a middle school dance. He was in the sixth grade and would have gladly stayed home that night. He was never one for dancing. But Bonnie felt it would be a good growing experience for him. Adolescents are more in the realm of her expertise. But from my church camp days, I knew how the middle school boys would build rock forts in the woods, while the girls would flirt with college counselors. And never the twain shall meet. So I had come early to rescue my boy.

It used to be much easier.

Upon arrival, one of Nathaniel's teachers informed me that, as per school policy, all parents were required to wait in the lobby until the conclusion of the dance. I did not protest. I had just sat down when Marty marched past, dressed in all camouflage from hat to boots, likely straight from his deer stand but who knows, really. The teacher politely informed him about the policies and procedures.

"The hell you say!"

Marty flung the poor man against the wall and rushed into the gym. That teacher grabbed a walkie-talkie and began speaking excitedly into it. Reassuring this red-faced young man that I was Brother Marty's pastor, I offered to fetch him and smooth things over.

I managed to enter the gym after all. The theme that year had something to do with Hollywood and the decorations resembled a movie set. I quickly spotted Nathaniel clustered with a few other boys his age in a corner about as far away from the dance floor as possible. They were backstage hands, lurking in the shadows. Center stage, right in the spotlight, was Marty's youngest girl—Delilah. She wore a red-sequined dress that sparkled as she twirled, dancing in the middle of a dozen eighth graders. The song ended and I half-expected those boys to ask for her autograph.

I heard my name. There was Marty, leaning against the wall. He had melted into the shadows like a hunter in the woods. I slipped over beside him as another song started. Even before I drew close, I could smell the alcohol.

"They sent you after me, huh, Wheeler?" His face was hidden under the cover of darkness, but I knew him well enough to hear the smile in his voice. "You know I didn't mean no harm, my brother." I suggested there might have been a better way to express his disagreement with school policy. He laughed. "You reckon I owe that teacher out there an apology?"

We watched Delilah for awhile. At an age when most kids seem all bony elbows and skinned knees, she was uncommonly graceful.

Marty spoke, just barely loud enough to be heard over the God-awful pop music blasting from the speakers.

"It ain't that I don't trust her. Lord knows, Delilah's got a good head on her shoulders. She's wise beyond her years."

He stepped into the light and turned to face me.

"Ain't nobody can tell me, I can't be where my kid is at."

Now, whenever I visit Marty, his leg is shackled to a wall. He has made his mistakes, but I wish to God I could change that. It is hard enough for families to stay together by their own free will.

Nathaniel. It's the dead of night. Nathaniel!

He called only a few minutes ago. Drunk. And hopped up on Ritalin or something else. God, it was surreal. A waking dream. A tear in the fabric of time and space. Nathaniel and me.

When Mom died in the car accident, Dad came home from the hospital, sat down, and told me the news. His eyes were red, but he did not cry. I completely lost it. I dropped to my knees, trembling, nearly vomiting. That was how Nathaniel sounded tonight. It took several heart-wrenching minutes before he could calm down enough for me to understand him.

"Dad, I'm sorry."

Son, stop crying. My father had spoken firmly. When I did not cease my blubbering, he put his hand underneath my chin and forced me to match his stare. *You've got to hold it together, son. You hear me? Hold it together!* His eyes were not unkind. This is what life had taught him and this is what he felt he should be teaching me. I choked down the tears and mumbled an apology. *Dad, I'm so sorry.* I have kept my vow to never cry in front of my father again.

"Dad, I'm so sorry."

Nathaniel, I should be apologizing to you.

"Dad, what should I do?" Nathaniel is writing his own story, but I think I know that feeling.

Losing my mother was more than I could hold. I was twelve years old, going on thirteen, and felt as if the sun had turned to darkness and the moon to blood. Everything had changed. My center did not hold. So I went searching for help in the same place my father had abandoned. *Well then, you can go without me. I'm never going to church again!* This was my father's infamous declaration.

Dad has kept his vow, even when I was married, even when I was ordained, even when I baptized and confirmed his only grandsons.

"Dad, where can I go?" I was listening to Nathaniel, yet also somewhere else.

The Moravian Church was the only congregation within walking distance of my house. I had never been before. I have no clue what went on that first Sunday. Only afterward did it register that Reverend Jennings was away on vacation and some stranger was in the pulpit. I sat numb in the sanctuary. My mind was a blank slate. I would come back to the moment and realize that the rest of the congregation had been standing. The older woman sharing a pew with me asked several times if I was alright. Her eyes were full of compassion. I could only reply *yes, ma'am, I'm fine*.

I bolted during the last hymn, stealing down the street enough to escape attention and still keep an eye on the parking lot. When the last car pulled away, I snuck back inside the sanctuary, which had been left unlocked. I crept down the center aisle, treading lightly on the brick floor in case someone was still around. I believed that no one, no matter how well-intentioned, could be of any use to me.

I stood underneath the wooden cross suspended from the ceiling. *How could my mother be dead? No Heavenly Father would allow such a Bad Thing to happen!* I slammed my fist down on the pulpit Bible. As the thump reverberated in the empty chapel, I collapsed lengthwise in the first pew and began to sob into the seat cushion. Even when the substitute preacher sat down beside me, I was helpless to rein in my grief.

That man never spoke one word as he rested his large hand on the back of my head. I have no concept of time. I might have cried for five or fifty-five minutes. Eventually, I felt hollowed out. There was nothing left inside. The preacher lifted his hand gently. I straightened up beside him and took a deep breath. He was looking up at the suspended cross.

"Bless you, my son."

Over the rest of my young adulthood, Reverend Jennings would teach me a great deal about Moravian history and Christian theology; yet that unnamed preacher left me feeling as though I had been washed clean by a good hard rain. Though there were no easy answers on that day long ago and there are rarely easy answers in any day ever, I was given hope. Not something ephemeral suspended from on high, but as real as sitting beside me.

We can be repaired.

"Bless you, my son."

I repeated those very words to Nathaniel over the phone, spanning the expanse of time and space and heartache.

"Bless you, my son."

It was surreal. Holy.

I need to end here because I really must go. I should have already left.

But I am now remembering when Nathaniel was still learning to talk. Something loud would startle him and prompt his cry. *Hold you, hold you!* Of course, I would immediately bend and scoop him up. Daddy will keep you safe. Lord knows, that promise was not mine to guarantee.

"*I wish I could hold you, Nathaniel!*" I had cried just moments after offering that blessing.

My son inhaled sharply. "Would you? *Would you?*"

I did not hear the mysterious voice of God. I did remember Marty at that middle school dance. *Ain't nobody can tell me, I can't be where my kid is at.* And I heard my mom.

Go, Jaime, go!

Marjorie answered on the second ring and shouted something like yes absolutely are you kidding of course she could handle the service no problem! Why she'd play a few more hymns in order to eat up a little more time. Even take requests! Give them people their money's worth.

"And you tell him we love him," she added. "You tell Nathaniel that we all love him. Especially me."

I gave a courtesy call to Oak because he hates surprises even more than late night phone calls. I had not planned on spilling the whole truth, but Bonnie was still throwing our things in a suitcase and—what the hell—I figured I might as well get used to the inevitable response from people like him. So I found myself telling Oak Arnold—of all people—that my son is gay and that he needed me. Right now. When Oak replied, there was not even the slightest hesitation in his voice.

"You are doing the right thing."

Finally, there was my call to Frank Powers. He listened. Told me not to give the sermon a second thought because, after all, there was always next week and, besides that, he was pretty sure I had been repeating the same sermon for years now. Something about a Moravian dog. I bet Jesus also knew the secret of quiet laughter.

"Love you, James."

Normally, he calls me Wheeler.

There she is now with the clarion blast of the car horn! Bonnie waits with coffee and snacks to ease the long drive ahead. I can see the glow of the car's headlights from here. She will be revving the engine at any minute.

Time to go.

27316705R00068

Made in the USA
Middletown, DE
15 December 2015